3012340

F

BOWEN, E.
Encounters

LAST
COPY.
Aug 91.

HERTFORDSHIRE COUNTY LIBRARY

This book is due for return on or before
the last date sho~~~~ ~~~ it may be renewed
by personal app~~~~
quoting date for
top of this label.

RENEWAL
INFORM-
ATION

Books in dem~~~~

L.32A   M20   672

D1491676

CENTRAL RESOURCES
LIBRARY
01707-281530

25

14 AUG 2002

- 1 FEB 1996

- 6 MAR 1999

4 AUG 2000

L 33

ENCOUNTERS

ENCOUNTERS

Early Stories by
ELIZABETH BOWEN

SIDGWICK & JACKSON · LONDON
1949

ALS CONN: CG096171-6

To M. J.

HERTFORDSHIRE
COUNTY LIBRARY
F.
3012340

PRINTED IN GREAT BRITAIN BY RICHARD CLAY AND COMPANY, LTD.,
BUNGAY, SUFFOLK.

Preface

THESE stories, my first published work, were written between the ages of twenty and twenty-two. Their arrangement here is that of the first edition of 1923, in which I had the help of Mr. Frank Sidgwick; the order happens to be, roughly, chronological, though I do not believe that either of us had that in mind. One story, 'Requiescat,' is certainly out of place, coming higher up in the index than several stories I know to be earlier. 'Requiescat' has a Lake Como scene, and I did not go to that part of Italy until (as it then seemed) fairly late on.

The greater part of *Encounters* was, therefore, written just less than thirty years ago. I must have re-read the book many times in the months after the first copy reached my hands: to have failed to be dazzled by the apotheosis into print would have been unnatural. (None of these stories had appeared before: any magazine editors with whom I experimented had rejected them.) Since that summer, I had not read the collection through as a whole until I undertook to write this Preface. I now hope I am old enough to be clear of those split, heated and complicated feelings which must surround for the writer his or her early work. All the same, can I, I ask myself, approach *Encounters* as dispassionately as if it were a collection by an unknown young writer sent to me for review? I fear not.

What I remember about the writing of these stories is, chiefly, the newness of the sensation of writing. It is, of course, to be doubted whether that sensation ever becomes familiar ; or, still more, whether the writer ought to desire that it should. The sensation of desperate and overweening enterprise, of one's entire being being forced to a conclusive ordeal, remains constant. What possibly does wear off—or, through familiarity become less acute —is that uncanny first sense of complicity with one's surroundings, the physical objects, sounds and lights and shades comprehensively known as 'the writing-table.' The room, the table, the convulsive and anxious grating of my chair on the floor were made hyper-significant for me, in those early days, by the fact that here were substantial witnesses to my crossing of the margin of a hallucinatory world.

My embarking upon my first story, 'Breakfast,'— *not* the first I had attempted, but the first I was to bring to its end—had the character of a last hope. I had already, at twenty, failed to be a poet, and was in the course of failing to be a painter. The scene was, the top of a house at Harpenden ; an attic of which the window was set high—only when I stood up could I see gardens, apple-trees, a blur of open country beyond. Between the sill of the window and the top of my table intervened a stretch of white wall-paper, lightly mapped by damp which must have percolated in through the outdoor tiling. This, as I sat at the table, was at eye-level. The short, rose-dotted curtains, which I had too often allowed to blow out into the rain, fretted over my head and smelled slightly musty. Now and then a voice from one of the gardens could be heard. The then Midland Railway main line ran at a right angle to the bottom of the road in which the house stood; from time to time an up or down express roared by; or, more disturbingly, a local train slowed down as it approached the station. I wrote by hand, as distinctly as was possible for me—as when at school, two or three years before, I had been making a fair copy of an essay. As the filling-up of sheet after sheet of my block continued, I had the sense of swinging between two worlds.

The importance to the writer of first writing must be out of all proportion to the objective value of what is written. It was perhaps more difficult then than now to disentangle what was *there*, on the page, from the creative excitement which had given it birth. There could be but one test of validity: publication. I know I shaped every line in the direction of the unknown arbiter; there was still the sensation of 'showing up' work. When I say that had I not written with the intention of being published I should not have written, I should add that I did not so much envisage glory as cry out for affirmation. Publication would be the sign that I was not mad; more than that, it was the necessary gateway to being read. I know that I wrote then with no less—though also with no more—difficulty than now: as an occupation writing pleased me, which made it suspect, but also killed me, which made it to be respected. The sensation of struggle was predominant. I saw no point in killing myself for the sake of anything that was not to be a reality. For me, reality was the books I had read—and I turned round, as I was writing, from time to time to look at those books existing, in their unassailable sphere of reality, in the shelves behind me. (This was my own room.) I had engaged, by writing a book myself, to extend the bounds of reality one stage more.

Decision to fall back upon the short story, on the part of a young person who was a poet *manquée*, would today seem obvious. In those days, the retreat was more uncertain; the position of the short story was anomalous. It was not yet—I think I am right in saying—recognised as 'a form.' There had appeared so far, that is to say, little constructive-critical interest in the short story's possibilities and problems. Any such interest as there may have been had not travelled my way—I could not have been farther out of the movement. I had not gone to a university; I had no part in any intellectual life. I had read widely, but wildly. I did not know the stories of Hardy or Henry James; I may have heard of Chekov; I had not read Maupassant because I imagined I could not read French. . . . With regard to the short story, Katherine Mansfield was not only to be the innovator but to fly the flag; since *Bliss* the short story has never been quite ignored. I read *Bliss* when I had completed that first set of my stories which were to make *Encounters* —then, admiration and envy were shot through by a profound dismay: I thought, 'If I ever am published, everybody will say I imitated her.' I was right: this happened.

Preface

Did I, then, in writing my early stories, think I was doing something without precedent? I am sure not. I had found examples, which were also incentives— Richard Middleton's *The Ghost Ship*, and E. M. Forster's *The Celestial Omnibus*. Those collections I read at school.

In themselves, the *Encounters* stories are a mixture of precocity and naïvety. I still cannot consider them badly written; the trouble with some of them is, they were not well found. But at twenty— twenty-one, twenty-two—where is one to find a story? Stories require people; and principally one is interested in oneself; or, it might be more true to say, one's own sensations. Those appear to be new; actually, what *is* new is one's awareness of them, and one's cultivation of that awareness for its own sake. Literature, in those years, excites one according to its power to reflect, express, altogether magnify awareness of which one is incoherently conscious in oneself. In my own case, it would not be too much to say that my attitude to the most noble literature was brigandish: I was waiting to rifle its vocabulary. I was also a pupil, possibly over-quick to be taught to see anything I had not so far seen for myself. I can perceive, now, in the *Encounters* stories how much I was using synthetic language to express something perfectly real to me.

I can see, too, how I was each time using the story as a device, in order to place sensations at one remove from me—and at once to exalt and rationalise them. The characters in the stories—are they, then, stand-ins, stooges? In the main, to them I was ungratefully harsh. It is the harshness and the touches of little-girlish smartie unkindness throughout *Encounters* which today shock me. These creatures, were they materialised that I might score off them ? Were there at work the malignancies of a protracted childhood ; or, had I debts to settle ? . . . It seems worth remarking (*a*) that with very few exceptions—the child in 'Coming Home,' the schoolgirls in 'Daffodils,' Laura in 'Sunday Evening'—all these characters were considerably older than myself, were involved in experiences of which I had no knowledge and often gutted by passions beyond my ken ; and (*b*) that not more than three of them bore resemblance to anybody I had encountered in real life. They all the more pleased me, I remember, by having an actuality for which I could not account. They impressed me, even while I mocked at them, by having experience that was none of mine.

I know that I had a snobbery with regard to age. For my generation (possibly the last of which this was true) grown-ups were the ruling class. As an only child I had lived very much among them, noted as closely as possible their ways, and tried in my reading to keep abreast with books they seemed to admire, which were of many sorts. Moreover, I was being continually shifted from household to household, in and out of varying social groups, to and fro between Ireland and England. This made me diplomatic, and imitative. All through my youth I lived with a submerged fear that *I* might fail to establish grown-up status ; and that fear had probably reached its peak when I started writing. A writer and a grown-up, it appeared to me, could not but be synonymous. I had embarked on an act of levelling-up. As far as I can see (more from these stories, re-read, than from my memory) I was anxious at once to approximate to the grown-ups and to demolish them. At the same time, I was not yet ready to try conclusions with any world I knew, particularly that of my own family. My characters, therefore, lived in houses which, in real life, I had done little more than contemplate from the outside.

The above could be called the social motive. Horror of being at a disadvantage may have worked itself out in my aptness to take my characters at a disadvantage, to snap them (in the camera sense) at moments when weakness, mistrust, falseness or affectation could not but be exposed. But, one point more : in fairness to the writer of *Encounters* one must allow for literary fashion, and for the psychological climate of a decade. The famous Twenties, mocking and disabused, had already set in, though had not yet a name. Though I did not meet writers, I keenly read what was being written. If I was *mal élevée* in my attitude to the human race, so were my betters.

The stories have build, style, and occasional felicities of expression which I must say startle me. Their strong point is, visual clarity ; and though there is too often a conscious, metallic clang of phrases, on the whole the meaning does not bog down in words. But I find in the best of them something better— an uncorrupted attempt to say something not said before. 'Daffodils,' 'Requiescat,' 'All Saints,' 'Mrs.

Windermere,' 'The Shadowy Third,' 'Sunday Evening' and 'Coming Home' engage my respect. As a performance, 'The Return' is the most showy, but it has a hollow kernel—a situation I thought up, or borrowed, rather than felt. The truest ring of emotion comes out of 'Coming Home'—which was transposed autobiography. 'Requiescat' and 'The Shadowy Third' make me, now, very clearly see how I used to work : I would posit a situation and then explore it. (Of that method a third, malignant example is 'The Evil that Men Do——')

I was still not clear, while I was writing *Encounters*, as to the distinction between a story and a 'sketch.' I failed to see that, while it could be emancipated from plot (in the magazine-formula sense), a story, if it is to *be* a story, must have a psychological turning-point. A sketch, lacking the turning-point, is little more than knowing, accomplished reportage—'Breakfast' and 'The Lover' are examples. When one or two reviewers described the published *Encounters* as 'a collection of sketches,' I felt this to be derogatory. Actually, it would have been correct to describe the volume as a collection of sketches and stories. I imagine few writers who are today at the age that I was then would have the same blind spot: story-consciousness has gone on maturing. All the same, the point seems just worth noting.

I claim for the *Encounters* stories one other virtue—susceptibility, rendered articulate, to places, moments, objects and times of year. This shows, at the best, with the naïvety of a deep love. 'Daffodils' overflowed from uncontainable pleasure in the

streets of St. Albans on one March afternoon;
'Requiescat' eased an obsession about Lake Como,
and a particular garden I knew above it. Even in
the centrally artificial 'Return,' I see the welling up
of a solitary person's love of an empty house; and
the scene, if not the characters, in 'The Shadowy
Third' seems to be dignified by emotion. Granted
all this, I see one reason for my springing upon my
characters at their most trying moments: their
susceptibilities had to be heightened to match my
own.

I owed the publication of *Encounters*—had it not
been published, what would have happened next?—
to three persons. In order of time they were—a
woman friend, the 'M. J.' of the dedication, who
paid the bill for having the stories typed; Rose
Macaulay, upon whose decision as to whether I was
or was not a writer I hung my future, and Frank
Sidgwick, to whom Rose Macaulay wrote. He not
only honoured me by his faith but made what had
appeared the most fantastic of my dreams come true
by bringing out *Encounters* in the same series as *The
Celestial Omnibus*. The title, which I think did much
to further the book, was of his finding.

ELIZABETH BOWEN.

April, 1949.

Contents

Breakfast

'BEHOLD, I die daily,' thought Mr. Rossiter, entering the breakfast-room. He saw the family in silhouette against the windows; the windows looked out into a garden closed darkly in upon by walls. There were so many of the family it seemed as though they must have multiplied during the night; their flesh gleamed pinkly in the cold northern light and they were always moving. Often, like the weary shepherd, he could have prayed them to keep still that he might count them.

They turned at his entrance profiles and three-quarter faces towards him. There was a silence of suspended munching and little bulges of food were thrust into their cheeks that they might wish him perfunctory good-mornings.

Miss Emily further inquired whether he had slept well, with a little vivacious uptilt of her chin. Her voice was muffled: he gathered that the contents of her mouth was bacon, because she was engaged in sopping up the liquid fat from her plate with little dice of bread, which she pushed round briskly with a circular movement of her fork. It was not worth sitting down till she had finished, because he would be expected to take her plate away. Why was the only empty chair always beside Miss Emily?

Last night in the lamplight he had almost begun to think he liked Miss Emily. She was the only lady present who had not beaten time with hand or foot or jerking head while they played 'Toreador Song' on the gramophone. But here, pressed in upon her by the thick fumes of coffee and bacon, the doggy-smelling carpet, the tight, glazed noses of the family ready to split loudly from their skins. . . . There was contamination in the very warm edge of her plate, as he took it from her with averted head and clattered it down among the others on the sideboard.

'Bacon?' insinuated Mrs. Russel. 'A *little* chilly, I'm afraid. I do hope there's plenty, but we early birds are sometimes inclined to be *rather* ravenous.'

She added: 'There's an egg,' but there was no invitation in her tone.

She could never leave a phrase unmodified. He could have answered with facetious emphasis that he was *almost* inclined to believe he would *rather* have enjoyed that egg.

Dumbly, he took two rashers of the moist and mottled bacon.

'And then,' Hilary Bevel was recounting, 'it all changed, and we were moving very quickly through a kind of pinkish mist—running, it felt like, only all my legs and arms were somewhere else. That was the time when *you* came into it, Aunt Willoughby. You were winding up your sewing machine like a motor car, kneeling down, in a sort of bunching bathing dress. . . .' She dared indelicacy, reaching out for the marmalade with a little agitated rustle to break up the silence with which her night's amazing experiences had been received.

Miss Emily, always kindly, tittered into her cup. She kicked the leg of Rossiter's chair and apologised; and he watched her thin, sharp shoulders shining through her blouse.

Mrs. Russel's eye travelled slowly round the table; there slowed and ceased the rotatory mastication of her jaws. Above her head was a square of white light reflected across from the window to the overmantel. He wished that the sheen of the tablecloth were snow, and that he could heap it over his head as that eye came round towards him.

'Now for it,' he braced himself, clenching his hands upon his knife and fork, and squaring his elbows till one touched Miss Emily, who quivered.

'I'm afraid you couldn't hardly have heard the gong this morning, Mr. Rossiter. That new girl doesn't hardly know how to make it sound yet. She seems to me just to give it a sort of *rattle*.'

Damn her impudence. She censored him for being late.

'Oh, I—I heard it, thank you!'

They had all stopped talking, and ate quite quietly to hear him speak. Only Jervis Bevel drained his coffee-cup with a gulp and gurgle.

'The fact is, I was—er—looking for my collar-stud.'

'Ah, yes. I'm afraid you've sometimes been a little reckless about buying new ones before you were quite sure you'd lost the others, haven't you, Mr. Rossiter? Only fancy,'—she looked round to collect the attention of the breakfasters; there was a sensation to follow—'Annie found *three* good ones, really good ones, under the wardrobe, when she was turning out your room.'

'I can't think how they get there,' he protested, conscious of inanity.

'Perhaps they took little legs unto themselves and walked,' suggested Hilary Bevel.

'Perhaps the wardrobe got up in the night and sat on top of them,' bettered Miss Emily.

There was a rustle of laughter, and she cast down her eyes with a deprecatory titter.

The remark was a success. It was really funny. It was received by Mrs. Russel with a warm benignity: 'Really, Emily, you do say silly things.' She laughed her gentle breathy laugh, gazing at Mr. Rossiter, who wriggled.

'I say—er—Bevel, when you've finished with that newspaper——'

Jervis Bevel looked insolently at him over the top of the paper. 'Sorry, I've only just begun. I left it lying on your plate some time, then I didn't think you'd have much time to read it, being rather rushed.'

Rossiter hated Bevel, with his sleek head. He was not aware that he was rushed. What business had Bevel got to tell him so?

'Well, when you *have* finished——'

Hilary Bevel was staring at him across the table as though she had never seen him before. She had eyebrows like her brother's, owl's eyebrows, and long-lidded, slanting eyes; and affected a childish directness and ingenuousness of speech which she considered attractive. Her scarlet, loose-lipped mouth curled itself round her utterances, making them doubly distinct.

'Mr. Rossiter's got another tie on, a *crimson* tie!' said Hilary Bevel.

Rossiter was instantly aware, not only of his tie but of his whole body visible above the table-edge. He felt his ears protruding fanwise from his head, felt them redden, and the blush burn slowly across his cheekbones, down his pricking skin to the tip of his nose.

Mrs. Russel's attention was temporarily directed from himself by a skirmish with Aunt Willoughby. The click of swords was audible to all.

'Oh, but you wouldn't, Aunt Willoughby. Not when they've got five or six rooms to settle up every day, you wouldn't. You see, with you, when poor uncle was alive, it was a different thing altogether. What I mean to say is, in proportion to the size of the family you had more of them, in a kind of way. It was a larger staff.'

'Ah then, Rosie, but what I always used to say, "You do what I expect of you and we won't expect any more than that. I'm reasonable," I used to say, "I won't expect any more than that." *Annie* could tell you that was what I used to say to her. As my dear husband used to say,' Aunt Willoughby raised her voice, anticipating an interruption, 'there are those that can get good work out of their servants and those that can't. We mustn't be set up about it; it's just a gift, like other gifts, that many haven't got.

6

I've had such a happy, *happy* home,' she sighed towards the attentive Miss Emily. 'Always so comfortable, it was.'

'Annie *is* a funny girl,' reflected Mrs. Russel; 'she said to me—of course I never take the things those girls say seriously—"I wouldn't go back to Mrs. Willoughby not for anything you might give me, I wouldn't." I said, "But she spoke so well of you, Annie," and she just wagged her head at me, sort of. She *is* a funny girl! Of course, I didn't ought to tell you, but it made me laugh at the time, it did really.'

'I came down on her rather *hard*,' admitted Aunt Willoughby swiftly. 'I was so particular, you see, and she *had* some dirty ways. Now I shouldn't wonder—when was it you lost those collar-studs, Mr. Rossiter?'

'I don't exactly remember,' said Rossiter, basely. He felt Mrs. Russel's approval warm upon him, but was sorry to have failed Aunt Willoughby, who, disconcerted, relapsed into irrelevancy.

Miss Emily harked back.

'Oh, Hilary, you are awful—why shouldn't he?'

'Well, I didn't say he shouldn't, I simply said it *was* one. They'll be jealous of you at the office, won't they, Mr. Rossiter?'

7

Mr. Rossiter, eyeing her contemplatively, supposed that Miss Bevel was a 'merry' girl.

'It may mean an *occasion* for Mr. Rossiter,' said Mrs. Russel from her Olympia behind the urn. 'You shouldn't draw attention to it, girls.'

The light glanced on Hilary's waved and burnished hair as she turned her head towards Aunt Willoughby.

'*Nobody* takes *any* notice of little me, when *I* go gadding, do they, Auntie! Why, it's all round the table in a minute if I come down with half an inch of new coloured cammie-ribbon sticking out above my jumper!'

'You wouldn't put it in at all if you didn't think it was going to notice,' remarked her brother, without raising his eyes from the *Daily Express*.

'I wouldn't put on anything at all if I was quite invisible, if that's what you mean!'

Miss Emily glanced apprehensively at the unshaken barricade of newspaper.

'Oh, Hilary, you are *awf*——'

Jervis had apparently not heard.

'Hilary!' said Mrs. Russel, 'I'm afraid you're shocking Mr. Rossiter!' She lingered on the name as though he were something delicious to eat.

'I believe,' thought Rossiter, 'they all want to marry me! Is this insight or delirium? P'raps not Aunt Willoughby, but——'

He appraised Jervis round the edge of the newspaper. Surely he was showier, more attractive? Why couldn't he divert some of their attentions; take on, say, Miss Emily and Mrs. Russel? Mrs. Russel was old enough to be the mother of either of them.

A hand shot out suddenly from behind the urn. Rossiter jumped.

'——had your second cup of coffee yet,' Mrs. Russel was saying. 'You look quite poetic, Mr. Rossiter'—she was referring to his abstracted glare—'Aren't you going to pass along your cup?'

'Thank you—*half* a cup, if you please.'

'There's no *hurry*.' She glanced over her shoulder at the round relentless clock-face on the mantel. 'You see, you eat rather faster than the others, Mr. Rossiter, though they have had a bit of a start this morning!'

Did he really bolt his food and make, perhaps, disgusting noises with his mouth?

'That's why I always say we'd rather breakfast early—all of us, even the ones who haven't necessarily got to rush. It's so much homier, one feels, than rough-and-tumble modern breakfast

9

nowadays. Everybody sort of rushing in and scrambling and snatching and making *grabs* at things off a table at the side. There's nothing so homely,' said Mrs. Russel with conscious brilliance, 'as a comfortable sit-down family to breakfast.'

'My God!' said Jervis irritably, 'there's going to be another strike on that damned railway—they're cutting down the trains again. Why *pretend* railways are a convenience—that's what I should like to know?'

No one could tell him.

He pushed his chair back from the table, impatiently, and crossed his legs.

'Pore old thing, then,' trilled Hilary. 'Diddums wazzums cwoss.'

'They're *not* taking off the eight-forty-seven, are they?'

'Not the eight-*forty-seven*?'

'They are. That means either the eight-twenty-seven or the eight-fifty-three. The *eight-fifty-three*!'

'The eight-twenty-seven,' they decided unanimously.

'Then that'll just have to mean breakfast earlier,' said Mrs. Russel brightly; 'you won't mind, will you, girls?' Her appeal included Aunt Willoughby, who made no response. 'You see, we couldn't hardly rush them over their breakfasts, could we?'

This was 'home comforts.' This was one of the privileges for which Rossiter paid her twenty-four shillings a week. Being sat round and watched while you were eating. Not being *rushed*. He had a vision of a 'rushed breakfast,' of whirling endlessly through space while one snapped at a sausage with little furtive bites; of munching bread and marmalade with the wind of one's velocity whistling through one's teeth.

Would it be better? Could it be worse?

Not worse than his chair-edge creaking against Miss Emily's; the unceasing consciousness of her unceasing consciousness of him. Not worse than Hilary Bevel, *vis-à-vis*; with her complacent prettiness, her tinkling, laboured witticisms. Not worse than Aunt Willoughby's baffled, bearded morosity; than Jervis Bevel's sleek disdain.

He would escape from Mrs. Russel, her advances, her criticisms, her fumbling arguments that crushed you down beneath their heavy gentleness until you felt you were being trampled to death by a cow. By a blind cow, that fumbled its way backwards and forwards across you. . . .

The 'girls' delivered their ultimatum in chorus.

'England expects,' declaimed Hilary, turning her eyes towards the ceiling, 'effery woman to—er—do—er herr dew-ty.'

'It's *nice* to be down early,' said Miss Emily earnestly, 'with a nice long day stretching out in front of me.'

'Breakfast will be at quarter to eight sharp,' said Mrs. Russel. 'Mr. Rossiter, we really must *try* not to lose our collar-studs.'

All his days and nights were loops, curving out from breakfast time, curving back to it again. Inexorably the loops grew smaller, the breakfasts longer; looming more and more over his nights, eating more and more out of his days.

Jervis Bevel's eyes swerved over to the mantelpiece. He pushed his chair back farther over the bristling carpet pile.

'Well,' he said, 'I think it's almost time——'

The room broke up, the table grew smaller again as they all rose from their chairs. Mrs. Russel and Aunt Willoughby gathered themselves together; Hilary seized Miss Emily by the back of the waist and punted her laughingly towards the door.

The coffee and the bacon and the hostility and the christian forbearance blew out before them into the chilly hall.

Daffodils

MISS MURCHESON stopped at the corner of the High Street to buy a bunch of daffodils from the flower-man. She counted out her money very carefully, pouring a little stream of coppers from her purse into the palm of her hand.

'——ninepence—ten—eleven—pence half-penny—*a shilling* ! Thank you very much. Good afternoon.'

A gust of wind rushed up the street, whirling her skirts up round her like a ballet-dancer's, and rustling the Reckitts-blue paper round the daffodils. The slender gold trumpets tapped and quivered against her face as she held them up with one hand and pressed her skirts down hastily with the other. She felt as though she had been enticed into a harlequinade by a company of Columbines who were quivering with laughter at her discomfiture; and looked round to see if anyone had witnessed her display of chequered moirette petticoat and the inches of black stocking above her boots. But the world remained unembarrassed.

To-day the houses seemed taller and farther

13

apart; the street wider and full of a bright, clear light that cast no shadows and was never sunshine. Under archways and between the houses the distances had a curious transparency, as though they had been painted upon glass. Against the luminous and indeterminate sky the Abbey tower rose distinct and delicate.

Miss Murcheson, forgetting all confusion, was conscious of her wings. She paused again to hitch up the bundle of exercise books slithering down beneath her elbow, then took the dipping road as a bird swings down into the air. Her mouth was faintly acrid with spring dust and the scent of daffodils was in her nostrils. As she left the High Street farther behind her, the traffic sounded as a faint and murmurous hum, striking here and there a tinkling note like wind-bells.

Under her detachment she was conscious of the houses, the houses and the houses. They were square, flat-faced and plaster-fronted, painted creams and greys and buffs; one, a purplish-rose colour. Venetian shutters flat against the wall broadened the line of the windows, there were coloured fanlights over all the doors. Spiked railings before them shut off their little squares of grass or gravel from the road, and between the railings branches swung

14

out to brush against her dress and recall her to the wonder of their budding loveliness.

Miss Murcheson remembered that her mother would be out for tea, and quickened her steps in anticipation of that delightful solitude. The silver birch tree that distinguished their front garden slanted beckoning her across the pavement. She hesitated, as her gate swung open, and stood looking up and down the road. She was sorry to go in, but could not resist the invitation of the empty house. She wondered if to-morrow would fill her with so strange a stirring as to-day. Soon, in a few months, it would be summer and there would be nothing more to come. Summer would be beautiful, but this spring made promise of a greater beauty than summer could fulfil; hinted at a mystery which other summers had evaded rather than explained. She went slowly up the steps, fumbling for her latch-key.

The day's dinner still hung dank and heavy in the air of the little hall. She stood in the doorway, with that square of light and sound behind her, craving the protection and the comfort with which that dark entrance had so often received her. There was a sudden desolation in the emptiness of the house.

Quickly she entered the sitting-room and

flung open the window, which set the muslin curtains swaying in the breeze and clanked the little pictures on the walls. The window embrasure was so deep that there was little light in the corners of the room; armchairs and cabinets were lurking in the dusk. The square of daylight by the window was blocked by a bamboo table groaning under an array of photographs. In her sweeping mood she deposed the photographs, thrust the table to one side, and pulled her chair up into the window. 'I can't correct my essays in the dark,' she asserted, though she had done so every evening of the year.

'How tight-laced you are, poor Columbines,' she said, throwing away the paper and seeing how the bass cut deep into the fleshy stems. 'You were brave above it all, but—there now!' She cut the bass and shook the flowers out into a vase. 'I can't correct,' she sighed, 'with you all watching me. You are so terribly flippant!'

But what a curious coincidence: she had set her class to write an essay upon Daffodils! 'You shall judge; I'll read them all out loud. They *will* amuse you.' She dipped her pen in the red-ink pot with an anticipatory titter.

With a creak of wheels a young woman went by slowly, wheeling a perambulator. She leant heavily on the handle-bar, tilting the perambulator on its two back wheels, and staring up, wide-mouthed, at the windows.

'How nice to be so much interested,' thought Miss Murcheson, pressing open the first exercise-book. 'But I'm sure it can't be a good thing for the baby.'

The essays lacked originality. Each paragraph sidled up self-consciously to openings for a suitable quotation, to rush each one through with a gasp of triumph.

> 'And then my heart with pleasure fills
> And dances with the daffodils.'

> 'Fair daffodils, we weep to see
> You fade away so soon.'

She wondered if any of her class could weep for the departure of a daffodil. Mostly they had disclaimed responsibility for such weakness by the stern prefix, 'As the poet says——.' Flora Hopwood had, she remembered, introduced a 'Quotation Dictionary,' which must have been round her circle.

'I must forbid it. Why can't they see things for themselves, think them out? I don't believe they ever really see anything, just accept things on the authority of other people. I could make them believe anything. What a responsibility teaching is—— But is it? They'd believe me, but they wouldn't care. It wouldn't matter, really.

'They're so horribly used to things. Nothing ever comes new to them that they haven't grown up with. They get their very feelings out of books. Nothing ever surprises or impresses them. When spring comes they get preoccupied, stare dreamily out of the windows. They're thinking out their new hats. Oh, if only I didn't know them quite so well, or knew them a little better!

'If I had a school of my own,' she meditated, running her eyes down the pages and mechanically underlining spelling-mistakes, 'I would make them think. I'd horrify them, if nothing better. But here—how ever can one, teaching at a High School? Miss Peterson would——

'They *do* like me. At least, one set does, I know. I'm rather a cult, they appreciate my Titian hair. They'd like me more, though, if I knew how to do it better, and knew better how to use my eyes. Their sentimentality embarrasses me. In a way they're so horribly mature, I feel at a disadvantage with them. If only they'd be a little more spontaneous. But spontaneity is beyond them at present. They're simply calves, after all, rather sophisticated calves.'

She dreamed, and was awakened by familiar laughter. Nobody's laughter in particular, but surely it was the laughter of the High School? Three girls were passing with arms close linked, along the pavement underneath her window. She looked down on the expressive, tilted ovals of their sailor hats; then, on an impulse, smacked the window-sill to attract their attention. Instantly they turned up three pink faces of surprise, which broadened into smiles of recognition.

'Hullo, Miss Murcheson!'

'Hullo, children! Come in for a minute and talk to me. I'm all alone.'

Millicent, Rosemary and Doris hesitated, eyeing one another, poised for flight. 'Righto!' they agreed unanimously.

Miss Murcheson, all of a flutter, went round to open the front door. She looked back at the sitting-room as though she had never seen it before.

Why had she asked them in, those terrible girls whom she had scarcely spoken to? They would laugh at her, they would tell the others.

The room was full of them, of their curiosity and embarrassment and furtive laughter. She had never realised what large girls they were; how plump and well-developed. She felt them eyeing her stack of outraged relatives, the photographs she swept off on to a chair; their eyes flitted from the photographs to the daffodils, from the daffodils to the open, red-scored exercise books.

'Yes,' she said, 'your writings, I daresay. Do you recognise them? I was correcting "Daffodils" and they made me dreary—sit down, won't you?—*dreary*. I wonder if any of you have ever used your senses; smelt, or *seen* things—— Oh, *do* sit down!'

She seemed to be shouting into a forest of thick bodies. They seated themselves along the edge of an ottoman in a bewildered row; this travestied their position in the class-room and made her feel, facing them, terribly official and instructive. She tried to shake this off.

'It's cruel, isn't it, to lie in wait for you like this and pull you in and lecture you about what you don't feel about daffodils!'

Her nervous laughter tinkled out into silence.

'It was a beastly subject,' said someone, heavily.

'Beastly? Oh, Mill—Rosemary, have you never seen a daffodil?'

They giggled.

'No, but looked at one?' Her earnestness swept aside her embarrassment. 'Not just heard about them—"Oh yes, daffodils: yellow flowers; spring, mother's vases, bulbs, borders, flashing past flower-shop windows"—but taken one up in your hands and felt it?'

How she was haranguing them!

'It's very difficult to be clever about things one's *used* to,' said Millicent. 'That's why history essays are so much easier. You tell us about things, and we just write them down.'

'That's why you're so lazy; you're using *my* brains; just giving me back what I gave you again, a little bit the worse for the wear.'

They looked hurt and uncomfortable.

Doris got up and walked over to the fireplace.

('Good,' thought Miss Murcheson, 'it will relieve the tension a bit if they will only begin to prowl.')

'What a pretty photograph, Miss Murcheson. Who is it? Not—not *you*?'

'*Me?*' said Miss Murcheson with amusement. 'Yes. Why not? Does it surprise you, then?'

'You've got such a *dinky* hat on!' cried the girl, with naïve astonishment.

The others crowded round her.

'You look so different,' said Doris, still scrutinising the photograph. 'Awfully happy, and prosperous, and—cocksure.'

'Perhaps it was the hat!' suggested Millicent.

'Oh, *Millicent*! No, I'm sure Miss Murcheson was *thinking* about something nice.'

'Or somebody.'

'Oh, Doris, you are awful!'

They all giggled, and glanced apprehensively across at her.

She wondered why she was not more offended by them.

'As a matter of fact,' she enlightened them, '*that* was because of daffodils. It just illustrates my point, curiously enough.'

They were still absorbed.

'Oh, Miss *Murcheson*!'

'*Miss* Murcheson!'

'When was it taken?'

'Last Easter holidays. Nearly a year ago. At Seabrooke. By a friend of mine.'

'*Do-oo* give me one!'

'——And me?'

'I'm afraid that's the only print I've got; and that's mother's.'

'Were there more?'

'Yes, various people took them. You see, I haven't faced a real camera for years, so when I got these snaps they were scrambled for by people who'd been asking me for photos.'

'People?' She was rising visibly in their estimation.

'Oh yes. Friends.'

'Why *daffodils*?' reverted Rosemary.

'Somebody had just given me a great big bunch.' She was impressed by their interest. 'I wonder if daffodils will ever make any of you look like that.'

'It all depends, you see,' said Millicent, astutely. 'Nobody has ever given us any. If they *did* perhaps——'

'*Really?*' said Miss Murcheson, with innocent concern. 'Take all those, if they would really inspire you! No, dears, I'd *like* you to.'

She gathered the daffodils together and lifted them, dripping, from the vase.

The girls retreated.

'Oh no, really, *not* your daffodils——'

'We don't mean——'

'Not *your* daffodils, Miss Murcheson. It wasn't *that* a bit.'

Evidently a false move on her part. She was bewildered by them; could not fathom the depths of their cinema-bred romanticism.

Doris had put away the photograph and stood with her back to the others, fingering the ornaments on the chimney-piece.

'There are lots of things,' she said rapidly, 'that you only feel because of people. That's the only reason things are there for, I *think*. You wouldn't notice them otherwise, or care about them. It's only sort of——' She stopped. Her ears glowed crimson underneath her hat.

'Association,' they sighed, ponderously.

'That's exactly what's the matter,' cried Miss Murcheson. 'We've got all the nice, fresh, independent, outside things so smeared over with our sentimentalities and prejudices and —associations—that we can't see them anyhow but as part of ourselves. That's how you're—we're missing things and spoiling things for ourselves. You—we don't seem able to *discover*.'

'Life,' said Doris sententiously, 'is a very big adventure. Of course we all see *that*.'

The other two looked at her quickly. All three became suddenly hostile. She was encouraging them to outrage the decencies of conversation. It was bad form, this flagrant discussion of subjects only for their most secret and fervid whisperings.

To her, they were still unaccountable. She had not wished to probe.

'I don't think that's what I meant,' she said a little flatly. 'Of course your lives will be full of interesting things, and those will be your own affairs. Only, if I could be able, I'm always trying, to make you care about the little fine things you might pass over, that have such big roots underground.

'I should like you to be as happy as I've been, and as I'm going to be,' she said impulsively. 'I should love to watch you after you've left my form, going up and up the school, and getting bigger, and then, when you've left, going straight and clearly to the essential things.'

The tassel of the blind cord tapped against the window-sill, through the rustling curtains they looked out on to the road.

They had awaited a disclosure intimate and personal. The donor of those last year's daffodils had taken form, portentous in their minds. But she had told them nothing, given them the stone of her abstract, colourless idealism while they sat there, open-mouthed for sentimental bread.

'Won't you stay to tea?' she asked. 'Oh, *do*. We'll picnic; boil the kettle on the gas-ring, and eat sticky buns—I've got a bag of sticky buns. We'll have a party in honour of the daffodils.'

The prospect allured her, it would be a fantastic interlude.

They all got up.

'Doris and Millicent are coming to tea with me, Miss Murcheson. Mother's expecting us, thanks most awfully. Else we should have loved to.'

'We should have loved to,' echoed the others. 'Thanks most awfully.'

She felt a poignant disappointment and relief, as standing with her eyes on the daffodils, she heard the children clattering down the steps.

To-morrow they will be again impersonal; three pink moons in a firmament of faces.

The three, released, eyed one another with a common understanding.

'Miss Murcheson has never really *lived*,' said Doris.

They linked arms again and sauntered down the road.

The Return

MR. and Mrs. Tottenham had come home.

The moist brown gravel of the drive and sweep bore impress of their fly wheels. Lydia Broadbent listened from the doorstep to the receding gritty rumble of the empty fly, and the click and rattle as the gate swung to. Behind her, in the dusky hall, Mr. Tottenham shouted directions for the disposal of the luggage, flustered servants bumped against each other and recoiled, and Porloch the gardener shouldered the heavy trunks with gasps and lurches, clutching at the banisters until they creaked.

Lydia heard Mrs. Tottenham burst open the drawing-room door and cross the threshold with her little customary pounce, as though she hoped to catch somebody unawares. She pictured her looking resentfully round her, and knew that presently she would hear her tweaking at the curtains. During her six weeks of solitude the house had grown very human to Lydia. She felt now as if it were drawing itself together into a nervous rigor, as a man draws himself together in suffering irritation at the entrance of a fussy wife.

'Were these all the letters, Lydia? I hope none were forwarded to Wickly? Porloch, do be careful of the paint! The fly was very stuffy, Lydia. I wish you'd ordered one of Bicklesfield's. His are always clean.'

Mrs. Tottenham had darted out of the drawing-room, swept up her letters from the table, and stood hesitating at the bottom of the stairs.

'You might order tea immediately. Yes, the drawing-room for to-day.' A red shimmer of firelight invited them through the open door. 'Herbert, *Her*-bert!'

Mr. Tottenham was clattering in the smoking-room. His face peered crossly at them round the door.

'I wondered if you had gone upstairs. Porloch has been very careless of the paint. You might have watched him, Lydia!' She vanished slowly into the gloom above.

Lydia went into the drawing-room and stood warming her hands before the fire. A servant with a lighted taper passed from gas-bracket to gas-bracket and the greenish lights sprang upwards in her wake. Outside the brown gloom deepened over the November garden. The young distorted trees loomed dark and sullen, the air was thick with moisture, heavy with decay.

To-day there had been no time to think.

Lydia was aware but dimly of a sense of desolation and of loss. Something was shattered that had built itself around her during these coherent weeks, something violated which had been sacred unawares. Every fibre of her quivered with hostility to these invaders who were the owners of the house. She was at odds with herself again, at odds with her surroundings. She stared at her gaunt reflection in the fireplace and knew that her best companion had drawn back again, forbidding her. She would be baffled once again by the hostility of Lydia Broadbent, her derision, her unsparing scorn. 'I was such friends with myself when they left us together; we were so harmonious and at ease with each other, me and myself and the house. Now we are afraid and angry with each other again.'

Mr. and Mrs. Tottenham were impossible. They were childless, humourless and dyspeptic. They were not even funny. There was nothing bizarre about them, or tragic or violent or farcical. They neither loved nor hated each other, there was nothing they did not know about each other; no mystery or fear between them. In the early days of their marriage they had been actively and articulately unhappy. She had had a lover; he had left her for months together and lived in some drab wickedness elsewhere. Then

her lover had deserted her, he had been left
more money; they had drifted together again,
bought 'The Laurels,' spun their shams and
miseries around them like a web and lurked
within them. They visited, were reputable and
entertained; and kept a home for Mr. Tottenham's nephew, their expectant heir.

'Lydia?'

The thin voice fluted over the banisters.
Lydia hurried upstairs, flicked at a panel of
Mrs. Tottenham's door and entered, her footsteps muffled among the woolliness of many
rugs. There was a blot of yellow light from a
candle on the writing-table. Mrs. Tottenham
stood beside the bed, staring at two sheets of
close-written paper and an envelope, which she
held out fan-wise between rigid fingers, as one
holding a hand at cards.

'Did—has my husband taken his mail yet?
Did he overlook the letters?'

'I think Mr. Tottenham's post is still lying on
the hall table. Is there anything you want to
show him?' They had all their correspondence
in common; it was quite impersonal.

'No, no, Lydia, shut the door, please. Is tea
up? It *is* draughty: I should have liked a fire.
You might get the things out of my dressing-
bag—there, it's over on the sofa.'

This constant attendance was to begin again. Lydia was well schooled to it; why had she forgotten?

She unpacked the combs and brushes, and Mrs. Tottenham fidgeted before the glass.

'Light the gas, please. I hate this half-light!' There was resentment in her glance towards the window, where the last daylight leaked in faintly through draperies of parchment-coloured lace. Why was Mrs. Tottenham so agitated, tugging her hat off and patting at her crimped and faded hair?

She bent to a level with the mirror; haggard-eyed and grinning with anxiety, she searched her bleached and baggy face to find what prettiness was there. Lydia watched her with apathetic curiosity from where, on her knees beside the sofa, she unwrapped the shoes and bottles from their little holland bags.

'Have you seen the photo,' asked Mrs. Tottenham suddenly, 'of me when I was twenty-five? On the chiffonier—the plush-framed one —you *must* know it!'

Lydia assented.

'It's a good one, isn't it? D'you think it's like me—now, I mean?'

'Quite a likeness, really, considering.'

'*Considering?*' (How sharp her voice was!)

'Oh, change of fashions makes a difference, doesn't it, and, well . . . time, of course.'

'Of course I know it wasn't taken yesterday, Lydia. *I* don't need telling. But I'm a lot younger than Mr. Tottenham to look at. There was a gentleman at the Hydro took us for father and daughter, really he did!'

Her voice was by turns peremptory, confidential, almost appealing. It died out into silence.

The room was restive and disturbed. 'Oh, you unhappy house,' thought Lydia. 'They have broken into your silence and given you nothing in return.'

'Tea will be ready, I think,' she reminded. Mrs. Tottenham turned sharply from the glass, and Lydia saw with amazement that she had reddened her lips. They shone with sticky brightness in her sallow face.

Mrs. Tottenham was conscious of her glance. 'Shows rather, doesn't it?' she queried diffidently, and rubbed her mouth with the back of her hand till the red was smeared out over her cheeks.

'One looks so washy after a journey. Just a touch of colour—one wouldn't notice it, hardly, if it wasn't for the glare.' Her muttered extenuations were not addressed to Lydia.

They heard the tea-tray rattling through the hall. Lydia turned the light out, and they prepared to descend. Mrs. Tottenham pawed her in the twilight. 'You needn't mention to Mr. Tottenham I've opened any of my letters. I'll be showing him the rest. This one was rather particular—from a friend of mine, it was.' An appeal still quavered in her husky tones which her paid companion had never heard before.

From the drawing-room they saw Mr. Tottenham scurrying across the grass, drawn teawards by the lighted window. There was something quick and furtive about him; Lydia had never been able to determine whether he dodged and darted as pursuer or pursued.

'Wretched evening, wretched.' He chattered his way across the crowded room. 'Been talking to Porloch—garden's in an awful way; shrubberies like a jungle. Did 'e sell the apples?'

He darted the inquiry at Lydia, turning his head sharply towards her, with his eyes averted as though he could not bear to look at her. At first she had imagined that her appearance repulsed him. She knew herself for a plain woman, but now she had learnt that he never looked at anybody if he could avoid it.

'Oh, he sold them well, I believe. I thought he wrote about them?'

'Oh yes, yes, sharp man, Porloch. Dickie been running round for his things?'

'Not often. He says he wants his letters forwarded to Elham till further notice.'

The reference to Elham tickled Dickie's uncle. He put his cup down, giggled, mopped at his mouth and darted a side glance at his wife.

Mrs. Tottenham was not listening. She sat very stiff and upright, staring straight before her, crumbling at her cake.

'Hey, Mollie! Dickie's gone to Elham. Didgehear that? Pore old Dickie's gone to Elham again! Never wrote and told me, never told me anything. The young dog!'

The silence was once more outraged by his falsetto giggles.

He held his cup out for Lydia to refill, and she watched with fascination the convulsive movements his throat made while he drank.

'Hey, Mollie! Don't forget we're going to the Gunnings to-morrow. Write it down, my dear girl, write it down, and tell them about orderin' the cab.' He always referred to Lydia obliquely as 'they' or 'them.'

'Gunnin's a good fellow,' he informed the fireplace.

'This cake is uneatable, Lydia. Wherever did you buy it?' Her grumble lacked conviction; it

34

was a perfunctory concession to her distrust of
her companion's housekeeping.

'Birch's. I'm sorry, Mrs. Tottenham. Aren't
you ready for more tea? It's nice and hot for
you, isn't it, after the journey?'

Lydia felt as though she had caught her own
eye, and was embarrassed and discomfited. She
listened with derision to her glib and sugary
banalities of speech. 'The perfect companion!'
taunted the hostile self. 'What about all those
fine big truths and principles we reasoned out
together? Yesterday we believed you were
sincere. *"Nice and hot after the journey."* Bah!'

The mirror in the overmantel now fascinated
Mrs. Tottenham. She finished her tea mechanically, laid her cup down and stood before the fireplace, patting and tweaking at her hair. Her
husband looked at her contemptuously. 'Pretty
little daughter I've got!' he mumbled, with his
mouth full of cake. It was a bitter comment on
the mistake made by the gentleman at the
Hydro.

Mrs. Tottenham put her hands before her face
and hurried from the room.

Lydia began to gather up the tea things, and
a servant darkened the windows with a musty
clatter of Venetian blinds. Mr. Tottenham's
chair creaked as he stretched his legs out to the

fire. The room was hot with the smell of tea and tea-cakes, and the smell of upholstery and wilting ferns was drawn out by the heat.

The hall outside was cold and quiet. The sense of the afternoon's invasion had subsided from it like a storm. Through a strip of door the morning-room beckoned her with its associations of the last six weeks. She saw the tall uncurtained windows grey-white in the gloom.

Her book lay open on a table: she shut it with a sense of desolation. It would never be finished now, it was too good a thing to read while *they* were in the house; to be punctuated by *her* petulant insistent chatter, *his* little shuffling, furtive steps. If only this room were all her own: inviolable. She could leave the rest of the house to them, to mar and bully, if she had only a few feet of silence of her own, to exclude the world from, to build up in something of herself.

If she did not go upstairs now Mrs. Tottenham would call her, and that, in this room, would be more than she could bear. Vaguely she pictured headlines: ' "Laurels" Murder Mystery. Bodies in a Cistern. Disappearance of Companion.' The darkness was all lurid with her visionary crime.

Mrs. Tottenham had not been round the

house. She did not say the rooms smelt mouldy, and she left the curtain-draperies alone.

Lydia wondered deeply.

'Did you know Sevenoaks?'

The question abashed her. What had Mrs. Tottenham to do with Sevenoaks?

'N—no. Scarcely. I've been over there sometimes for the day, from Orpington.'

'A friend of mine lives there—a Mr. Merton. He wrote to me to-day. He's come back from the Colonies and bought a place there. It's funny to hear from an old friend, suddenly. It makes me feel quite funny, really.'

She did not sound funny. Her voice was high-pitched with agitation. Lydia had been told all about Mrs. Tottenham's friends, and seldom listened. But she did not remember Mr. Merton.

'He wants to come and see us. I really hardly like, you know, to suggest the idea to Mr. Tottenham.'

'I thought you'd all your friends in common. How well these night-dresses have washed! They must have laundered nicely at the Hydro.'

'Ah, but this is different, you see.' She laughed a little conscious laugh. 'Mr. Merton was a particular *friend* of mine. I—Mr. Tottenham didn't used to know him.'

'I see,' said Lydia vaguely. 'A friend of yours before your marriage.'

'Well, no. You see, I was very young when I was married. Quite an inexperienced young girl—a child, you might almost say.'

Lydia supposed that Mrs. Tottenham *had* been young. She strained her imagination to the effort.

'I did very well for myself when I married Mr. Tottenham,' the wife said sharply. 'I must say I never was a fool. My mother'd never brought me up to go about, but we did a good deal of entertaining at one time, Mr. Tottenham's friends and my own, and we always had things very nice and showy. But it was a lonely life.'

Mrs. Tottenham's confidences were intolerable. Better a hundred times that she should nag.

'So you liked the Hydro—found it really comfortable?'

'Oh yes. But it's the coming back—to this. . . . Lydia, you're a good sort of girl. I wonder if I ought to tell you.'

'Don't tell me anything you would regret,' said Lydia defensively, jerking at the drawer-handles.

'You see, Mr. Merton was a good deal to me at one time; then we tore it, and he went off to

Canada and married there. I heard he'd been unhappy, and that there was the rumour of a split. Of course he didn't write or anything; we had ab-so-lutely *torn* it; but I couldn't help hearing things, and she seems to have been a really bad sort of woman—there were children, too. He's bringing the children back with him to Sevenoaks.

'He wants to come and see me. He's been thinking about me a great deal, he says, and wondering if I've changed, and wishing— He always was a straight sort of man; it was only circumstances drove him crooked. I daresay I was a good bit to blame. I've kept his photograph, though I know I didn't ought, but I liked having it by me to look at.'

She had unlocked a drawer and held a stiff-backed photograph up beneath the light, scrutinising it. Lydia listened to a distant surge of movement in the house beneath her; steps across the oil-cloth, windows shutting, voices cut off by the swinging of a door. She felt, revoltedly, as though Mrs. Tottenham were stepping out of her clothes.

'He says he's hardly changed at all. Seventeen years—they go past you like a flash, he says, when you're working.'

'Seventeen years,' said Lydia deliberately,

39

'are bound to make a difference to a woman. Did you care for him?'

Mrs. Tottenham made no answer; she was staring at the photograph. Her eyes dilated, and she licked her lips.

'I suppose you'll be glad to see him again?' suggested Lydia. She felt suddenly alert and interested, as though she were watching through the lens of a microscope some tortured insect twirling on a pin.

Mrs. Tottenham sat down stiffly on the sofa, and laid the photo on her lap. Suddenly she clasped her hands and put them up before her eyes.

'I couldn't,' she gasped. 'Not after all these years I couldn't. Not like this. O Lord, I've got so ugly! I can't pretend—I haven't got the heart to risk it. It's been so real to me, I couldn't bear to lose him.

'It's all gone, it's all gone. I've been pretending. I used to be a fine figure of a woman. How can I have the heart to care when I couldn't keep him caring?'

'You broke it off. It was all over and done with, you told me so. It was wrong, besides. Why should either of you want to rake it up when it was all past and done with seventeen years ago?'

'Because it *was* wrong. It's this awful *rightness* that's killing me. My husband's been a bad man, too, but here we both are, smirking and grinning at each other, just to keep hold of something we neither of us want.'

Lydia was terrified by the dry, swift sobbing. She felt suddenly hard and priggish and immature. All her stresses, her fears and passions, were such twilight things.

Mrs. Tottenham stood upright and held the photograph in the flame of the gas jet, watching the ends curl upwards. For all her frizzled hair and jingling ornaments and smudgy tentative cosmetics she was suddenly elemental and heroic.

It was over.

Lydia went quietly out of the room and shut the door behind her.

The place was vibrant with the humanity of Mrs. Tottenham. It was as though a child had been born in the house.

The Confidante

'You are losing your imagination,' cried Maurice.

It was a bitter reproach. He stood over her, rumpling up his hair, and the wiry tufts sprang upright, quivering from his scalp.

Penelope gulped, then sat for a moment in a silence full of the consciousness of her brutality. She had never dreamed that her secret pre-occupation would be so perceptible to Maurice. Unconsciously she had been drawing her imaginations in upon herself like the petals of a flower, and her emotions buzzed and throbbed within them like a pent-up bee.

The room was dark with rain, and they heard the drip and rustle of leaves in the drinking garden. Through the open window the warm, wet air blew in on them, and a shimmer of rain was visible against the trees beyond.

'I never meant——' began Penelope.

'I beg your pardon,' said Maurice stiffly. 'I suppose I am becoming quite insufferable. I have been making perfectly unjustifiable demands on your sympathy and patience and——

imagination. I am an egotistical brute, I daresay. Of course there is not the slightest reason
why you——' His indulgence intimated that
there was, on the contrary, every reason why
she should. . . . 'I felt a bit *jarred* just now,' he
excused himself, with simple pathos.

'I never meant, a bit——' resumed Penelope.

'I know, I know,' said Maurice, all mag-
nanimity. The sickly sweetness of this recon-
ciliation overpowered her.

'What a pair of fools we are!' she cried hys-
terically. 'Maurice, dear, we're wearing this
thing thin. I'm afraid I've been doing gallery to
you and Veronica for the last six months, and
you've both played up to me magnificently.
But——'

'Veronica——' protested Maurice.

'Oh, yes, Veronica comes here too. She
comes and sits for hours over there, just where
you are now. There's not an aspect of your
emotional relationship that we've not discussed.
Veronica's coming here this afternoon,' she said
abruptly. 'She's a chilly person. I'd better light
the fire.'

'God!' said Maurice.

Penelope was on her knees before the fireplace, her head almost inside the grate. Her
voice came hollowly from the dark recess.

'I thought you'd be surprised,' she said. ('Damn, it will *not* light!')

'Surprised!' said Maurice. 'Penelope'—his tone had the deadly reasonableness of a driven man's—'I think you hardly realise what you're doing. I know you meant well, my good girl, but really—— It puts us in such an impossible position. Surely you must see.'

'I see quite well,' she assured him. 'You and she both breathe and have your being in an atmosphere of conspiracy; it's your natural element, of course. To force you into the straighter, broader courses of the uncomplex would be as cruel as to upset a bowl with gold-fish in it and leave them gasping on the table-cloth. Ooh!' She sat back on her heels and ruefully beheld her grimy fingers.

Maurice tried his hardest to endure her. She heard him breathing heavily.

'It's really quite *unnecessary* to have a fire,' she soliloquised. 'But it makes a point in a room, I always think. Keeps one in countenance. Humanises things a bit. Makes a centre point for——'

She became incoherent. Maurice's irritation audibly increased. They were both conscious of the oppression of the darkening, rain-loud room.

'You're forcing our hands rather,' said Maurice.

'Forcing you into the banality of meeting each other sanely and normally in my drawing-room, with no necessity to converse in allusions, insinuations, and *doubles-entendres*? With me blessing you both and beaming sympathetically on you from afar? Bullying you into that?. . .

'I'm sorry!' she flashed round on him, impenitently.

'You don't understand,' he winced, and looked round him for his hat. 'I think it would be best for me to go.'

'I suppose I mustn't keep you,' she conceded with polite reluctance. 'But I think you really ought to see Veronica. She has—she will have something of particular importance to say to you. I shall go, of course.'

'Oh, don't!'

'But surely——?'

'There's nothing we can keep from you. And it makes it easier for both of us—as things are.'

'But do you never want to be alone with her?'

Maurice considered.

'I don't believe,' said Penelope, swiftly, 'that you two have ever been alone together for a second since your—acquaintanceship—began.'

45

'No,' said Maurice, sombrely. 'There have always been outsiders.'

'Audiences,' murmured Penelope.

'I beg your pardon?'

'Oh, nothing. Well, you'll be alone this afternoon. I'm going out,' she said with firmness.

'But don't you *understand*?'

'Oh, I understand the strain will be colossal —would have been. But there've been developments—suddenly. Veronica'll have a great deal to tell you. Has it never occurred to you she might get free after all? There'll be heaps to say,' she said, significantly.

'For heaven's sake——!' He threw up his hands again and paced the room in agitation, stumbling over stools.

'That was why I pulled up just now,' she continued. 'Seemed hard, perhaps, apathetic and unsympathetic when you were talking all that about awfulness, refined irony, frustration, and things. I was thinking how soon you'd—if you only knew—— And then you told me I was losing my imagination.'

'For which I have already begged your pardon,' said Maurice, patiently.

Penelope rose from the hearthrug and threw herself on to the Chesterfield. Maurice turned to her with a goaded expression, and she regarded him with shining eyes. Then the door opened with a jerk, and Veronica entered stiffly, with a rustle of agitation.

Maurice drew back into the shadow, and Veronica hesitated for a moment in the centre of the room, then groped out her hands towards Penelope, as though she could see little in this sudden gloom.

'Tell me,' she cried, without preliminaries, 'you, you heard from Victor?'

Penelope, who had risen, glanced across at Maurice. He took his cue.

'Veronica!' he quavered huskily.

Veronica's shoulders twitched. She turned on him in the dusk like a wild thing, with an expression that was almost baleful.

'You!' she said.

'Er—yes,' admitted Maurice. 'I'd simply no idea that I should . . . I just came in. By chance, you know.'

'It's just as well, isn't it?' interposed Penelope. 'We've—you've simply got to talk things out, Veronica; tell him. Show him Victor's letter.' She moved towards the door.

'Don't go!' shrieked Veronica. 'You've got to explain to him. I can't,' she said, with the finality of helplessness.

47

The rain had stopped, and through a sudden break in the clouds the watery sunshine streamed across the garden. Veronica sat down on an ottoman facing the window, and Penelope knelt beside her, looking at her pitifully.

The long, pale oval of her face was marred and puckered by emotion, fair hair lay in streaks across her forehead, her clothes were glistening from the rain. Many tears had worn their mournful rivulets through the lavish powder on her nose. Her gloved hands lay across her lap, in one was clutched a sheet of blue-grey notepaper. She would not look at Maurice, but turned pathetic eyes on Penelope and made appeal with soundless moving lips.

'Veronica has had a letter from Victor,' said Penelope, slowly and distinctly. 'He releases her from her engagement. He says . . . he explains. . . . He is not so blind as you both seem to have thought, and he has seen for some time that Veronica was not happy. He has noticed that she has been listless and preoccupied, and has interpreted her unhappiness—rightly! He is convinced, he says, that Veronica has ceased to care for him, but that she is too scrupulous, or not quite brave enough perhaps, to speak out and make an end of things herself. He knows that her affections are elsewhere, and he believes

48

that he is doing the best thing he can for her by setting her free.'

Veronica had turned a little, and sat facing Maurice. Penelope saw the golden flicker of her lashes; the blue letter fluttered to the ground from between her writhing fingers.

'The trousseau was all bought,' she faltered. 'The going-away dress came from Pam's this morning, just before I got that letter.'

Penelope could not speak; she felt utterly inadequate. Maurice shifted his position; and stood leaning up against the window-frame; with intensity of interest he turned his head and looked into the garden.

'It's stopped raining,' he observed. Veronica did not move; but Penelope saw her eyes slide sideways, following his movements under drooping lids.

'How do you know all this,' Maurice asked abruptly, 'what Victor says and that, when you've had no time to read his letter?'

'He wrote to me, too,' said Penelope. She heard her own voice, self-conscious and defiant.

'To *you*! Why you?'

'But we know each other—rather well. Since much longer than he's known Veronica. And, well, you see I'm her cousin. He thought I'd make things easier for her. Do the explaining as

far as possible. Probably he thought I'd speak
to you.'

She stealthily touched her pocket and smiled
to feel the crisp thick letter-paper crackle beneath her hand. Then she wondered if the
sound were audible to the others, and glanced
guiltily from one to the other of them. But they
sat there silent, embarrassed, heavily preoccupied, one on either side of her.

'So now——,' she said with bright aggres-
siveness. She could have shaken them.

'I do not think,' said Veronica, in a small
determined voice, 'that I am justified in accept-
ing Victor's sacrifice.'

'He is extraordinarily generous,' said Maurice,
without enthusiasm.

'The loneliness,' went on Veronica, gazing
wide-eyed down some terrible vista. 'Picture it,
Penelope, the disappointment and the blankness
for him. I could never have loved him, but I
would have been a good wife to him.' (Her
voice rose in a crescendo of surprise. She
thought 'How genuine I am!') 'We—we had
made so many plans,' she faltered; fumbled,
found no handkerchief, and spread her hands
before her face.

Penelope gave a little gasp, half sympathetic.
She was praying hard for tact.

'Veronica,' she said, 'I don't think you should let that stand between you and Maurice. You mustn't be too soft-hearted, dear. I don't think Victor's altogether unhappy. He's relieved, I know. You see, the last few weeks have been an awful strain for him, as well as—other people.'

'How do you know?'

'He told me.'

'You've been discussing me. Oh, Penelope, this is intolerable!'

'He had been talking to me; he had no one else. For a long time, I suppose, he put me in the position of a sister-in-law.'

'That was going too far!' cried Maurice. 'Had you neither of you the slightest idea of loyalty to Veronica?'

Penelope ignored him. She leant suddenly forward, crimson-cheeked, and kissed Veronica.

'Oh, my dear,' she said, 'did you think that because you couldn't care about Victor nobody else could? Do you expect him to go on giving you everything when you've got nothing to give him?'

They looked at her, dazzled by a flash of comprehension. When she rose from between them she left a gap, a gap she knew to be unbridgeable for both. They were face to face with the hideous simplicity of life. She had upset their bowl and left the two poor gold-fish gasping in an inclement air.

'Now at last you two have got each other,' she cried, smiling at them from the threshold. 'Nothing more to bother or disturb you. Just be as happy and as thankful as you can!'

They sat in silence till the last ironical echo died away. Then *'Don't go!'* they cried in unison.

But she was gone.

Requiescat

MAJENDIE had bought the villa on his honey-moon, and in April, three months after his death, his widow went out there alone to spend the spring and early summer. Stuart, who had been in India at the time of Howard Majendie's death, wrote to Mrs. Majendie before starting for home and her reply awaited him at his club; he re-read it several times, looking curiously at her writing, which he had never seen before. The name of the villa was familiar to him, Majendie had been speaking of it the last time they dined together; he said it had a garden full of lemon trees and big cypresses, and more foun-tains than you could imagine—it was these that Ellaline had loved. Stuart pictured Mrs. Ma-jendie walking about among the lemon-trees in her widow's black.

In her letter she expressed a wish to see him —in a little while. 'I shall be returning to Eng-land at the end of June; there is a good deal of business to go through, and there are several things that Howard wished me to discuss with you. He said you would be willing to advise and help me. I do not feel that I can face England

53

before then; I have seen nobody yet, and it is difficult to make a beginning. You understand that I feel differently about meeting you; Howard wished it, and I think that is enough for both of us. If you were to be in Italy I should ask you to come and see me here, but as I know that you will be going straight to Ireland I will keep the papers until June, all except the very important ones, which I must sign without quite understanding, I suppose.' In concluding, she touched on his friendship with Howard as for her alone it was permissible to touch. Stuart wired his apologies to Ireland and planned a visit to the Italian lakes.

Three weeks afterwards found him in the prow of a motor-boat, furrowing Lake Como as he sped towards the villa. The sky was cloudless, the hills to the right rose sheer above him, casting the lengthening shadows of the afternoon across the luminous and oily water; to the left were brilliant and rugged above the clustered villages. The boat shot closely under Cadenabbia and set the orange-hooded craft bobbing; the reflected houses rocked and quivered in her wake, colours flecked the broken water.

'Subito, subito!' said the boatman reassuringly and Stuart started; he did not know that his impatience was so evident. The man shut off his engines, let the boat slide farther into the shore, and displacing Stuart from the prow, crouched forward with a ready boat-hook. They were approaching the water-stairway of the villa.

For a few moments after he had landed, while the motor-boat went chuffing out again into the sunshine, Stuart stood at the top of the stairway looking irresolutely through the iron gates. He was wondering why he had come to Italy, and whether he even cared at all for Mrs. Majendie. He felt incapable of making his way towards her under the clustered branches of those trees. If there had been a little side-gate it would have been easier to go in; it would not have been so difficult, either, if he had ever been here with Howard Majendie. But this was *Her* place; she had loved it because of the fountains.

He pushed open the big gate, already cold in the shadow, and followed the upward curve of the avenue among the lemon-trees. Beyond the villa disclosed itself, unlike all that he had expected; he was surprised at his own surprise and did not realise till then how clearly he must have visualised it. There was a wide loggia, a flight of steps, a terrace on a level with the loggia running along the side of the hill. Cypress-trees rose everywhere, breaking up the view. He passed under the windows, climbed the steps and crossed the loggia, not looking to left or right for fear that he might see her suddenly, or even one of her books. The loggia had an air of occupation; it was probable that on any of those tables, or among the cushions, he might see her book, half open, or the long-handled lorgnettes that Majendie had given her in France.

The servant said that Mrs. Majendie was in the garden. She showed Stuart into a tall, cool parlour and disappeared to find her mistress. Stuart, distracted by a scent of heliotrope, made an unseeing circle of the room; he was standing before a Florentine chest when the girl came back with a message. Mrs. Majendie would see him in the garden. It would have been easier to meet her here; he had pictured them sitting opposite to one another in these high-backed chairs. He followed the girl obediently out of the house, along the terrace, and down a long alley between hedges of yew. The white plume of a fountain quivered at the end, other fountains were audible in the garden below. He could hear footsteps, too; someone was approaching by another alley that converged with his beyond the fountain. Here they met.

She was less beautiful than he had remembered her, and very tall and thin in her black

56

dress. Her composure did not astonish him; her smile, undimmed, and the sound of her voice recalled to him the poignancy of his feelings when he had first known her, his resentment and sense of defeat—she had possessed herself of Howard so entirely. She was shortsighted, there was always a look of uncertainty in her eyes until she came quite near one, her big pupils seemed to see too much at once and nothing very plainly.

'I never knew you were in Italy,' she said.

He realised that it would have been more considerate to have written to prepare her for his visit.

'I came out,' he said, 'quite suddenly. I had always wanted to see the Lakes. And I wanted to see you, but perhaps I should have written. I—I never thought . . . It would have been better.'

'It doesn't matter. It was very good of you to come. I am glad that you should see the villa. Are you staying near?'

'Over at Varenna. How beautiful this is!'

'The lake?'

'I meant your garden.' They turned and walked slowly back towards the house. 'I hope I didn't take you too much by surprise?'

'Oh no,' she said. It almost seemed as though

she had expected him. 'Yes, it is beautiful, isn't it ? I have done nothing to it, it is exactly as we found it.'

They sat down on a stone bench on the terrace, looking a little away from one another; their minds were full of the essential things impossible to be said. Sitting there with her face turned away from him, every inch of her had that similitude of repose which covers tension. His lowered eyes took in her hands and long, thin fingers lying against the blackness of her dress. He remembered Howard telling him (among those confidences which had later ceased) how though he had fallen in love with the whole of her it was her hands that he first noticed when details began to detach themselves. Now they looked bewildered, helpless hands.

'I took you at your word,' he said; 'I wanted to help; I hoped there might be something I could do, and in your letter——'

'I took you at your word in asking for help. There is a great deal I must do, and you could make things easier for me, if you will. I shall be very grateful for your help about some business; there are papers I must sign and I don't understand them quite. There were things that Howard had never explained.' She looked full at him for a moment and he knew that this was the first time she had uttered her husband's name. It would be easier now.

'He had told me everything,' he said quickly, as though to intercept the shutting of a door. 'I was always to be there if you should need me— I had promised him.' She must realise that she owed him nothing for the fulfilment of a duty. He thought she did, for she was silent, uttering no word of thanks.

'Why did you so seldom come and see us?' she asked suddenly. 'Howard had begun to notice lately, and he wondered.'

'I was in India.'

'Before you went to India.' A little inflection in her voice made him despise his evasion.

'There is a time for all things, and that was a time for keeping away.'

'Because he was married?'

Stuart did not answer.

'We wanted you,' she said, 'but you didn't understand, did you?'

She did not understand, how could she? She must have discussed it all, those evenings, with the Majendie that belonged to her; he had not understood either.

'I was mistaken, I suppose,' he said. 'I—I should have learnt later.'

There was a slight contraction of her fingers,

and Stuart knew that he had hurt her. If he hurt her like this a little more, it would probably be possible to kill her; she was very defenceless here in the garden that Majendie had bought her, looking out at the unmeaning lake. He had crowded out all tenderness for her, and her loneliness was nothing but a fact to him.

'There were messages for you,' she said, turning her head again.

'Were there?'

'He said——,' her lips moved, she glanced at him a little apprehensively and was silent. 'I have written down everything that he said for you. And I believe he left you a letter.'

'Can you remember the messages?' he asked curiously.

'I wrote them down; I have them in the house.' She looked at him again with that short-sighted intensity; she knew every word of the messages, and with an effort he could almost have read them from her eyes.

'Did he expect to see me?'

'Yes, once he knew that he was ill. He knew that you could not possibly leave India before April, but he kept on—expecting. I wanted to cable to you and he wouldn't let me. But I know he still believed, above all reason, that you'd come.'

60

'If I'd known, if——'

'You think I should have cabled without telling him?' She thought he blamed her and she evidently feared his anger. Curious . . . He had been so conscious of her indifference, before; he had been a person who did not matter, the nice friend, the family dog—relegated. It was that that had stung and stung. After all he need never have gone to India, it had been a resource of panic. It had saved him nothing, and there had been no question of saving *her*. He wondered why she had not cabled; it was nothing to her whether he went or came, and Howard's happiness was everything.

'Yes, I wonder you didn't cable.'

'I am sorry; I was incapable of anything. My resource was—sapped.'

He looked at her keenly; it was a doctor's look.

'What have you been doing since?' he asked (as the medical man, to whom no ground was sacred). 'What are you going to do?'

'I was writing letters, shutting up the house. And here I'm trying to realise that there's nothing more to do, that matters. And after-wards——'

'Well?'

'I don't know,' she said wearily; 'I'd rather not, please. . . . Afterwards will come of itself.'

He smiled as now he took upon himself the brother-in-law, the nice, kind, doggy person. 'You should have somebody with you, Ellaline. You should, you owe it to yourself, you owe it to'—he realised there was no one else to whom she owed it—'to yourself,' he repeated. 'You must think, you must be wise for yourself now.'

She looked, half-smiling, at him while he counselled. He had never achieved the fraternal so completely.

'It's not that I don't think,' she said. 'I think a great deal. And as for wisdom—there is not much more to learn once one has grown up. I am as wise as I need be—"for myself." '

'When are you going back to England?'

'If you would do one or two things for me I needn't go back until the autumn.'

'You can't stay here all the summer.'

'No,' she said, looking round at the cypresses —how pitiful she was, in Howard's garden. 'They say I couldn't, it would be too hot; I must go somewhere else. But if you could help me a little this autumn I could finish up the business then.'

'I may have to be in Ireland then.' He tore himself away from something brutally, and the brutality sounded in his voice.

She retreated.

'Of course,' she said, 'I know you ought to be there now—I was forgetting.'

Because he was a person who barely existed for her (probably) she had always been gentle with him, almost propitiatory. One must be gentle with the nice old dog. It was not in her nature to be always gentle, perhaps she had said bitter things to Howard who mattered to her; there was a hint of bitterness about her mouth. At himself she was always looking in that vague, half-startled way, as though she had forgotten who he was. Sometimes when he made a third he had found her very silent, still with boredom; once or twice he had felt with gratification that she almost disliked him. He wondered what she thought he thought of her.

Now it was the time of the Angelus, and bells answered one another from the campaniles of the clustered villages across the lake. A steamer, still gold in the sun, cleft a long bright furrow in the shadowy water. The scene had all the passionless clarity of a Victorian water-colour.

'It is very peaceful,' Stuart said appropriately.

'Peaceful?' she echoed with a start. 'Yes, it's very peaceful . . . David' (she had called him this), 'will you forgive me?'

'Forgive you?'

63

'I think you could understand me if you wished to. Forgive me the harm I've done you. Don't, don't hate me.'

How weak she was now, how she had come down! 'What harm have you done to me?' he asked, unmoved.

'You should know better than I do. I suppose I must have hurt you, and through you, Howard. An—an intrusion isn't a happy thing. You didn't give me a chance to make it happy. You came at first, but there was always a cloud. I didn't want to interfere, I tried to play the game. Now that we've both lost him, couldn't you forgive?'

'I'm sorry I should have given you the impression that I resented anything—that there was anything to resent. I didn't know that you were thinking that. Perhaps you rather ran away with a preconceived idea that because you married Howard I was bound to be unfriendly to you. If you did, you never showed it. I never imagined that I had disappointed you by anything I did or didn't do.'

'It was not what you didn't do, it was what you *weren't* that made me feel I was a failure.' (So *that* was the matter, he had hurt her vanity!)

'A failure,' he said, laughing a little; 'I thought you were making a success. If I didn't

64

come oftener it was not because I did not think
you wanted me.'

'But you said just now——'

'A third is never really wanted. I had set my
heart on seeing Howard happy, and when I
had, I went away to think about it.'

'Oh,' she said hopelessly. She had guessed
that he was putting her off. 'Shall we walk a
little down the terrace? There is a pergola
above, too, that I should like you to see.' She
was taking for granted that he would not come
to the villa again.

They rose; she stood for a moment looking
irresolutely up and down the terrace, then took
a steeper path that mounted through the trees
towards the pergola. Stuart followed her in
silence, wondering. The world in her brain was
a mystery to him, but evidently he had passed
across it and cast some shadows. For a moment
he almost dared to speak, and trouble the peace
of the garden with what had been pent up in
him so long; then he knew that he must leave
her to live out her days in the immunity of
finished grief. The silence of imperfect sympathy would still lie between them, as it had
always lain; his harshness could no longer cast a
shadow in her world, that was now as sunless as
an evening garden. His lips were sealed still,

and for ever, by fear of her and shame for his dead loyalty to Howard. The generosity of love had turned to bitterness within him, and he was silent from no fear to cause her pain.

'Beautiful,' he said, when they reached the pergola and could look down on lake and garden through the clustered roses.

'Will you be long at Varenna?'

'I don't expect so, no. Some friends want me to join them on Lake Maggiore, and I think of going on to-morrow afternoon.'

'That will be better,' she said slowly. 'It *is* lonely seeing places alone—they hardly seem worth while.'

'I'm used to it—I'm going back to India in six months,' he said abruptly.

'Oh, I didn't know.' Her voice faltered. He had not known himself till then. Her face was whiter than ever in the dusk of the pergola, and her hands were plucking, plucking at the creepers, shaking down from the roses above white petals which he kept brushing from his coat.

'I'm sorry you're going back,' she said. 'Everybody will be sorry.'

'I won't go until I have finished everything that I can do for you.'

An expression came into her eyes that he had

66

never seen before. 'You have been a friend,' she said. 'Men make better things for themselves out of life than we do.'

'They don't last,' he said involuntarily.

'I should have said that so far as anything is immortal——' He watched a little tightening of her lips.

'It takes less than you think to kill these things; friendship, loyalty——'

'Yours was unassailable, yours and his'; she spoke more to herself than to him. 'In those early days when we three went about together; that time in France, I realised that.'

'In France?' he said stupidly.

'Yes. Don't you remember?'

He remembered France; the days they had spent together, and the long evenings in star-light, and the evening he had strolled beside her on a terrace while Majendie tinkered with the car. It was a chilly evening, and she kept drawing her furs together and said very little. The night after, he had lain awake listening to her voice and Majendie's in the next room, and making up his mind to go to India.

'Yes,' he said. 'Now, will you let me have the papers and we could go through them now? I could take any that are urgent back to town with me; I shall be there in a week.'

She twisted her hands irresolutely. 'Could you come to-morrow, before you go? I would have them ready for you then, if you can spare the time. I'm tired this evening; I don't believe I would be able to understand them. Do you mind?'

'No, of course not. But may I come in the morning? I am going away early in the afternoon.'

She nodded slowly, looked away from him and did not speak. She was evidently very much tired.

'I think I ought to go,' he said after a pause.

'If you hurried you could catch that steamer down at Cadenabbia.'

'Then I'll hurry. Don't come down.'

'I won't come down,' she said, holding out her hand. 'Good-bye, and thank you.'

He hurried to the end of the pergola, hesitated, half turned his head, and stopped irresolutely. Surely she had called him? He listened, but there was no sound. She stood where he had left her, with her back towards him, leaning against a pillar and looking out across the lake.

Turning, he pushed his way between the branches, down the overgrown path. The leaves rustled, he listened again; somebody was trying to detain him. As the slope grew steeper he quickened his steps to a run, and, skirting the terrace, took a short cut on to the avenue. Soon the lake glittered through the iron gates.

She leant back against the pillar, gripping in handfuls the branches of the climbing rose. She heard his descending footsteps hesitate for a long second, gather speed, grow fainter, die away. The thorns ran deep into her hands and she was dimly conscious of the pain. Far below the gate clanged, down among the trees. The branches of the roses shook a little, and more white petals came fluttering down.

All Saints

THE Vicar moved about the chancel in his cassock, thoughtfully extinguishing the candles. Evensong was over, and the ladies who had composed the congregation pattered down the aisle and melted away into the November dusk. At the back of the church somebody was still kneeling; the Vicar knew that it was the emotional-looking lady in black waiting to speak to him as he came down to the vestry; he feared this might be a matter for the confessional and that she might weep. The church was growing very dark; her black draperies uncertainly detached themselves from the shadows under the gallery. As he came down towards her, her white face looked up at him, she made a rustling movement and half rose. A curious perfume diffused itself around her, through the chilly mustiness of the pew.

She murmured a request; the Vicar bowed his head. 'I will wait for you in the church porch,' she said in a clear voice with a suggestion of a tremolo. 'Perhaps we could walk across the churchyard?'

He hurried to the vestry with the sense of a reprieve.

She was waiting in the porch with her hands clasped, and smiled anxiously at the Vicar, who turned to lock the door behind him.

'Such a beautiful church!' she said as they walked on together.

'We consider it very beautiful.'

'How the people must love it.' Her manner was very childlike; she half turned to him, shyly, then turned away.

'Would you like another window?'

'A window?'

'A coloured window for the Lady Chapel. I would love to give you a window.' She made the offer so simply that the Vicar felt as though he was being offered a kitten.

'But, my dear lady, windows like that are very expensive.'

'I know,' she said eagerly, 'but I would be quite able to afford one.'

'A—a memorial window?'

'Memorial?'

'Of some relation or dear friend who has passed over?'

'Oh no,' she said vaguely, 'I know so many people who have died, but I think none of them would care about a window.'

'Then you have no particular purpose?'

'I think coloured windows are so beautiful. They make one feel so religious and good.'

The Vicar was nonplussed; he wished to say a great deal to her but did not know how to begin. Her ingenuousness half touched and half offended him. She was not young, either; he could hardly explain her to himself as young. Yet standing up so straight among the slanting tombstones she had no congruity with the year's decline; the monotone of twilight, the sullen evening with its colourless falling leaves rejected her; she was not elderly, he thought. She was perennial, there was that about her that displeased the Vicar; she was theatrical. Having placed her, he felt more at ease.

He said: 'I will place your very kind offer before the Vestry,' and took a few steps in the direction of the lych-gate. She looked up at him with fine eyes that she had once learnt how to use; she was so little conscious of the Vicar's masculinity that he might have been one of the tombstones, but eyes that have learnt their lesson never forget.

'Must you go at once?' she said pathetically. 'I want to talk a little more about the window. I would like to go and look from outside at the place where it is going to be.'

72

They retraced their steps a little and took a path that skirted the north side of the church and passed underneath the two east windows.

'I know you are not a resident,' said the Vicar. Still a diffident man, he disliked these inquiries; however oblique, they savoured too strongly of parsonic officiousness. But still, one ought to know.

'Do you think of paying us a long visit? The country is hardly at its best just now. Do you like the village?'

'I think the village is sweet—it does appeal to me. So quaint and homely. I am staying here in lodgings; they are most uncomfortable, but I sleep well, and the eggs are fresh. And then I love the country. My real name is Mrs. Barrows.'

'Do you intend a long stay?' repeated the Vicar, trying not to feel that her last sentence was peculiar.

'I want to watch them putting up the window. After that, I don't know. I don't think I could bear to be long away from London. Perhaps I might buy a cottage here, if you would help me.'

Evidently she was a person of means.

'This is the Lady Chapel window,' said the Vicar suddenly.

'Oh,' she cried in consternation. 'I did not know it was so small. We must make it larger—I think this would never hold them.'

'Hold whom?'

'All Saints—I want it to be an All Saints window. I went to church last Thursday; I heard the bells ringing and went in to see. I thought perhaps it was a wedding. I found a service, so I stayed, and you were preaching an All Saints Day sermon. It was beautiful; it gave me the idea. You said "called to be saints" was meant for all of us; I'd never heard of that idea. I'd thought the saints were over long ago; I'd seen old pictures of them when I was a child. I thought yours was a beautiful idea. It helped me so.'

'It is not only an *idea*, it is quite true.'

'I know. But it was beautiful of you to think of it.'

'Oh dear, oh dear, oh dear,' said the Vicar, half aloud.

'But then, of course, I supposed there must still be saints. And I thought of two or three people, then of quite a number. Ladies I have met, who have affected me—most strongly—and one dear boy I know——'

'We have most of us been privileged——'

'Don't you think,' she said, with round eyes,

'that saints must often seem quite unconventional?'

'In so far as conventionality is error—yes.'

'There,' she cried, 'I knew you'd agree with me. Wouldn't you describe a saint as somebody who, going ahead by their own light——'

'By a light that is given them——'

'That's what I meant—doesn't care what anybody says and helps other people; really makes it possible for other people to go on living?'

'Well, yes.' The Vicar hesitated over this definition.

'Don't saints seem always very strong?'

'There is a great strength in them, but there is weakness too; they have a great deal in themselves to combat before——'

'Before they can fight other people's battles.'

'Nobody can fight another's battle! We have got to fight our battles for ourselves—against ourselves.'

'Oh,' she said a little flatly, 'now that wasn't my idea. When I'm in a difficulty, or even in the blues, I just go to one of these friends of mine and talk it out, and, well, it's quite extraordinary the difference I feel. I see light at once. It's as if they took a burden off my shoulders.'

'There is only One who can do that. Can't you try and get straight to the Divine?'

Her voice out of the darkness—it was now very dark—sounded lonely and bewildered.

'No, I don't seem to want to. You see, I'm not at all good.'

'All the more reason——'

She ignored the interruption. 'It's power; that's what some people have; they're what I call good people—saints. And you know, these friends I was talking about; they're not at all conventional and they never go to church, except, perhaps, to weddings. And one or two of them are—oh, *very* unconventional. You'd be surprised.'

They walked across the churchyard, just able to see the path by the reflected light on the wet flagstones. The Vicar tried to help her: 'And you find that contact with certain personalities brings with it healing and invigoration?'

She grasped eagerly at the phrase. 'Healing and invigoration, yes, that's what I mean. It isn't anything to do with love or friendship. When I was younger I thought that loving people was meant to help one; it led me—oh, so wrong. Loving is only giving, isn't it? Just a sort of luxury, like giving this window. It doesn't do you any good, or the person either.

But people like ——'—she named a notorious lady—'I can't tell you how she's helped me. She's so brave, nobody seems too bad for her. She never despises you. And I've another friend who is a spiritualist.'

'Error!'

'She told me all about myself; she was so wonderful, her eyes went through and through. She said, "You're going the wrong way," and then it all came to me. She helped me so. And another who was a missionary's wife——'

This seemed simpler, but he wondered what he could get at behind it all.

'She didn't live with him. She had met him first at a revivalist meeting; she said he was too wonderful, but he couldn't have been as wonderful as her. She used to come and see me in the mornings, when I was in bed; I was very lonely then, a dear friend and I had just parted. She never talked religion, but there was something wonderful about her face.'

'And all this has really helped you? Force of example——'

'I don't want to copy them: I only want to know they're there.'

'What holds you in them isn't of themselves.'

'Isn't it?'

'It's simply a manifestation.'

77

She failed to understand him.

'They are able to help you—that is their privilege and God's will. But they can't do everything.'

'They do, you see; they see I can't do anything to help myself, and I suppose there must be a great many other people like me. They get at something I can't reach and hand it down to me—I could put it like that, couldn't I? That's what saints have always done, it seems to me.'

'Nobody was ever meant to be a go-between,' he said with energy. 'You've simply no conception——'

'I get everything I want that way,' she said placidly. 'I'm a very weak sort of person, I only want to be helped. Saints are the sort of people who've been always helping people like me; I thought I'd like to put up a window as a sort of thank-offering to them. Crowds and crowds of people I wanted to put in, all with those yellow circles round their heads, dressed in blue and violet—I think violet's such a beautiful colour. And one big figure in the foregound, just to look like helpfulness, holding out both hands with the look I've sometimes seen on people's faces. When can I know for sure about the window? I mean, when will you tell me if they'll let me put it up?'

'I don't know,' said the Vicar, agitatedly, hurrying towards the lych-gate and holding it open for her to pass through. 'I'll come round and see you about it. Yes, I know the house.'

'Oh, would you?' she said, shyly. 'Well, that would be kind. You know, talking about helpfulness, you're one of that sort of people. You don't know what it's meant to me to hear you preaching. You'd hardly believe——'

'Good-night,' said the Vicar abruptly. He raised his hat, turned on his heel, and fled through the darkness. . . .

The New House

COMING up the avenue in the February dusk
he could see the flash and shimmer of firelight
through the naked windows of the library. There
was something unearthly in those squares of puls-
ing light that fretted the shadowy façade, and
lent to the whole an air of pasteboard unreality.

The scrunch beneath his feet of the wet
gravel brought his sister to the doorstep.

'*Herbert*!' she cried, 'oh, do come in and see it
all. You've been such ages to-day—what *were*
you doing?'

'Your messages,' he said; 'they delayed me.
That stupid fellow at Billingham's had made a
muddle over those window measurements for
the blinds; I had to go over to the workshop and
give the order personally.'

Standing in the hall, he was surprised to hear
his voice ring out into spaciousness.

'I never realised how big it was,' he said with
gratification. 'Why, Cicely, you're all in the
dark. You might have lighted up and made the
place look a bit more festive. It's all very well to
hear how big one's house is, but I'd like to see it
with my own eyes.'

'I'm sorry,' said Cicely; 'as a matter of fact I'd only just come in myself. I was out in the garden.'

'*Gardening?*'

'No. Just poking about. You never heard anything like the way the thrushes sing. I never knew before they could sing like that. Or perhaps I'd never had time to listen. And the snowdrops are coming out all along the kitchen garden border. Oh, Herbert——'

'I shouldn't have thought that a house-move was exactly the most leisurely time to listen to thrushes. But of course——!'

'But I *had* been working.'

His injured dignity was impenetrable, like a barrier of steel. She turned aside from it with a shrug.

'Come in and see what I have done. The library—— *Janet*!' she called down a dark archway. 'Janet, *tea*! The master's in.'

Down the far end of the long room was an open fireplace. His chair was pushed up to the fire and an impromptu tea-table covered with newspaper had been set beside it. His books were stacked in piles against the walls, and their mustiness contested with the clean smell of scrubbed and naked boards.

'A nice room,' said Herbert. 'On Sunday I

shall have a good long day at the picture-hanging. I can't have these windows, Cicely; they're quite indecent. Haven't you even got a dust sheet to pin up across them? Any tramp——'

'I'll see. There won't be much light, though, anyhow. The man was in to-day about the fittings, and he says they won't be able to turn the gas on at the main till to-morrow afternoon. We shall have to do our best by candle-light. I've got some ready.'

She folded paper into a spill and lighted a long row of candles, ranged in motley candlesticks along the chimney-piece.

'Tut-tut,' said Herbert. 'We shall find it very difficult to work. How tiresome these people are.'

'Yes,' said Cicely.

He resented her tone of detachment. She had blown out her spill and stood twisting the charred ends of paper between her fingers. Long streaks of hair had loosened themselves and hung across her forehead, her cheeks were smeared with dust, her tall thin figure drooped with weariness, but her eyes were shining in the firelight with a strange excitement.

She became conscious of his irritated scrutiny.

'I must be looking simply awful——'

82

'Yes,' said Herbert.

'I'd better try and tidy before tea.'

'Yes. If we *are* going to have tea. If it doesn't come at once I really can't be bothered. There's a great deal for me to do, and *I* can't afford to waste any time.'

He was a hungry man and peevish, having snatched a hasty and insufficient lunch. He thought that he detected a smile of indulgence as she raised her voice and shouted:

'Janet—*hurry*!'

They heard Janet stumbling up the three steps from the kitchen. She entered with the squat brown tea-pot, one hand splayed against her heart.

'Such a house!' she gasped. 'It's that unexpected, really it is!'

They ate in silence. All Herbert's old irritation with his sister surged up within him. She was such a vague, uncertain, feckless creature; the air of startled spirituality that had become her as a girl now sat grotesquely on her middle-aged uncomeliness. He contrasted her with the buxom Emily. Emily would have known how to make her brother comfortable. But, of course, Emily had married.

She spoke.

'I suppose I might take mother's furniture. It

really is mine, isn't it? Just that little work-table, and the book-shelf, and the escritoire.'

'I don't see what you mean by "*take* it." It'll all be in the same rooms, in the same house as the rest. Of course, poor mother gave them to you. But I don't see how that makes any difference. I was thinking we might put that little escritoire in the drawing-room. It will look very well there.'

Cicely was silent.

Herbert brushed the crumbs out of the creases in his waistcoat.

'Poor mother,' he unctuously remarked.

'Come and see the house,' said Cicely—she was aware that her quick speech shattered what should have been a little silence sacred to the memory of the dead—'come and see what you'd like to begin on, and what Janet and I had better do to-morrow. We got the bedrooms tidy, but your basin and jug are odd, I'm afraid. The cases of crockery haven't arrived yet——

'I haven't got a basin and jug at all,' she said defensively.

Every step of Herbert's through the dis-ordered house was a step in a triumphal pro-gress. Every echo from the tiles and naked boards derided and denied the memory of that small brick villa where he and Cicely had been

84

born, where their mother's wedded life had begun and ended; that villa now empty and denuded, whose furniture looked so meagre in this spaciousness and height.

He carried a candlestick in either hand and raised them high above his head as he passed from room to room, peering round him into corners, looking up to moulded cornices and ceilings.

Standing in the big front bedroom he saw himself reflected in the mirrored doors of a vast portentous wardrobe, and beamed back at his beaming, curiously-shadowed face. Behind him he saw Cicely seat herself on the edge of the wire mattress, and place her candle carefully beside her on the floor. The mahogany bedroom suite loomed up round them out of the shadows. She sensed his radiant satisfaction with relief.

'It *is* a lovely house,' she said. 'Oh, Herbert, I do hope you're going to be happy!'

'I hope we both are,' he amended kindly. 'We must have some people staying, Cicely. The Jenkins, and that lot. Entertain a bit—after all, my dear girl, we can afford it now!'

He was glad when she did not seem to realise how their circumstances had bettered—it gave him the opportunity for emphatic reminders.

They passed out on to the landing, and stood

85

looking down into the depths of the well-staircase.

'I'm sure mother did want us both to be happy,' said Cicely, peering over the banisters. Herbert felt eerily as though she were deferring to the opinion of some unseen presence below them in the darkness.

'Of course she wished us the best, poor mother.' He clattered a little ostentatiously past her down the stairs.

'She would have loved this house!' Her voice came softly after him, and he heard her limp hand slithering along the banister-rail.

'Damn the gas-man,' he muttered, feeling his way across the hall, where his candle-flames writhed and flickered in a draught. It was enough to give anyone the creeps, thus groping through an echoing, deserted house with a ghost-ridden, lackadaisical woman trailing at his heels. If only they'd had the gas on.

Cicely was a fool: he'd teach her!

At the root of his malaise was a suspicion that the house was sneering at him; that as he repudiated the small brick villa so the house repudiated him; that Cicely and the house had made a pact against him, shutting him out.

He was so bourgeois and no parvenu. He, Herbert Pilkington, was good enough for any

86

house bought with his own well-earned money. He pushed savagely against the panels of the drawing-room door.

This was the largest room in the house. A pale light fell across the floor from the scoops of two great bow-windows, and there was a glimmer in the mirrors—fixtures—panelling the walls.

Herbert put down his candles and stood back in admiration.

'Next year,' he said, 'we will buy a grand piano; it would look well there, slanting out from that corner.

'The shutters—we ought to shut the shutters.' Fussily he wrestled with the catches. For all his middle-aged precision he was like a child delirious over some new toy.

'It needs children; it's a room for children,' said Cicely, when the clatter had subsided.

Something in her tone filled him with a sense of impropriety. She was gripping the edges of the chimney-piece and staring down into the grate. Her knuckles stood out white and strained.

'Herbert, Richard Evans wrote to me again yesterday. To-day I answered him. I—I am going to be married.'

Sitting on the Chesterfield, Herbert scrutinised his boots. He heard his voice say:

'Who is going to see about the furniture?'

His mind grappled with something immeasurably far away.

Cicely repeated, 'I am going to be married.'

Suddenly it flashed across him: he was full of angry light.

'Married!' he shouted, '*married—you*!'

'I thought it was too late,' she whispered, ''till quite lately. Then, when mother went, everything was broken up; this move came—all my life I seem to have been tied up, fastened on to things and people. Why, even the way the furniture was arranged at No. 17 held me so that I couldn't get away. The way the chairs went in the sitting-room. And mother. Then, when I stayed behind to see the vans off; when I saw them taking down the overmantels, and your books went out, and the round table, and the sofa, I felt quite suddenly "I'm free." I said to myself, "If Richard asks me again——" But I thought he must be tired of asking me. I said, "If only he asks me again I can get away before this new house fastens on to me." '

With her stoop, her untidiness, her vagueness and confusion, her irritating streaks of mysticism, he wondered: Could any man find her desirable?

He remembered Richard Evans, thin and jerky and vaguely displeasing to his orderly mind; with his terrible spasms of eloquence and his straggly moustache. He had come in often when they were at No. 17 and sat for hours in the lamplight, with his shadow gesticulating behind him on the wall.

'Nobody needs me,' she was saying. 'Nobody wants me, really, except him. I see it now, and I've got to——'

'What about *me*? Don't *I* count? Don't *I* need you? What about all these years; the housekeeping?' His voice rose to a wail, 'and what the devil am I to do about the move?'

'Of course I'll see you through the move. Really, Herbert——'

'I've been a good brother to you. We've got along very well; we've had a happy little home together all these years, haven't we, and now poor mother's gone——'

His eloquence choked him. He was stabbed by the conviction that she should be saying all this to him. Instead she stood there, mulishly, hanging down her head.

'You're too old to marry,' he shouted; 'it's—it's *ridiculous*!'

'Richard doesn't think so.'

'You don't seem to realise you're leaving me alone with this great house on my hands, this great *barn* of a house; me a lonely man, with

89

just that one silly old woman. I suppose Janet 'll go off and get married next! Nobody's too old to marry nowadays, it seems.'

'No,' she said with placid conviction. 'You'll marry, of course.'

'*Marry—me?*'

She turned to look at him, pink, self-confident, idiotically pretty.

'But of course. That's what I've been feeling. While I was here—— Men are so conservative! But this is no sort of life for you really, Herbert; you want a wife, a pretty, cheery wife. And children——'

'Children!'

'Oh, don't shout, Herbert. Yes, you don't want the family to die out, do you, after you've made such a name for it, done such fine big things?'

He felt that two springs were broken in the sofa, and pressed the cushions carefully with his hand to discover the extent of further damage.

'Damn it all,' he said querulously, 'I can't get used to another woman at my time of life!'

'Herbert, you've got no imagination.' Her tone was amused, dispassionate. She was suddenly superior, radiant and aloof; his no longer, another man's possession.

Her speech chimed in with his thoughts.

'Every man's got to have one woman!'

Taking one of the candles, she turned and left the room.

He sat there almost in the darkness; putting one hand up he fidgeted with his tie. Sleeking down his hair he smiled to find it crisp, un-thinned and healthy.

Slowly and cumbrously the machinery of his imagination creaked into movement.

He saw the drawing-room suffused with rosy light. Chairs and sofas were bright with the sheen of flowered chintzes, hung about with crisp and fluted frills. Over by the fire was the dark triangle of a grand piano; the top was open and a woman, with bright crimpy hair, sat before it, playing and singing. 'A pretty, cheery wife.' There was a crimson carpet, soft like moss, and a tall palm shadowed up towards the ceiling. Muffled by the carpet he heard the patter of quick feet. The little girl wore a blue sash trailing down behind her, and there was a little boy in a black velvet suit. They could do very well without Cicely's escritoire.

Lunch

'AFTER all,' said Marcia, 'there are egoists and egoists. You are one sort of egoist, I am the other.'

A ladybird had dropped on to her plate from a cluster of leaves above, and she invited it on to her finger and transferred it very carefully to the rail of the verandah.

'Differentiate,' said the stranger, watching the progress of the ladybird.

They were lunching on the verandah, and the midday sun fell through a screen of leaves in quivering splashes on to the table-cloth, the elusive pattern of Marcia's dress, the crude enamelled brilliance of the salad in a willow-pattern bowl, the dinted plate and cutlery slanting together at angles of confusion. The water was spring water, so cold that a mist had formed on the sides of their tumblers and of the red glass water-jug. They considered helpings of cold lamb, and their heads and faces were in shadow.

Through the open window the interior of the coffee-room was murky and repellent; with its drab, dishevelled tables, and chairs so huddled *tête-à-tête* that they travestied intimacy. It was full of the musty reek of cruets and the wraiths of long-digested meals, and of a brooding reproach for their desertion whenever they turned their heads towards it. A mournful waitress, too, reproached them, flicking desultorily about among the crumbs.

From under the verandah the hotel garden slanted steeply down to the road; the burning dustiness beneath them was visible in glimpses between the branches of the lime-trees. Cyclists flashed past, and an occasional motor whirled up clouds of dust to settle in the patient limes. Behind their screen of leaves they two sat sheltered and conversant, looking out to where, beyond the village, the country fell away into the hot blue distances of June, and cooled by a faint wind that crept towards them through a rustle and glitter of leaves from hay-fields and the heavy shade of elders.

The jewels flashed in Marcia's rings as she laid down knife and fork, and, drumming with her fingers on the table, proceeded to expatiate on egoists.

'Don't think I'm going to be clever,' she implored him, 'and talk like a woman in a Meredith book. Well, quite baldly to begin with, one acknowledges that one puts oneself first, doesn't

one? There may be other people, but it's ourselves that matter.'

He had relaxed his face to a calm atten-
tiveness, and, leaning limply back in his
chair, looked at her with tired, kindly eyes,
like the eyes of a monkey, between wrinkled
lids.

'Granted, if you wish it for the sake of argu-
ment. But——'

'But you are protesting inwardly that the
other people matter more? They do matter
enormously. But the more they matter to you,
still the more you're mattering to yourself; it
merely raises your standard of values. Have you
any children?'

'Six,' said the tired man.

'I have three,' said Marcia. 'And a husband.
Quite enough, but I am very fond of them all.
That is why I am always so glad to get away
from them.'

He was cutting his lamb with quiet slashing
strokes of his knife, and eating quickly and
abstractedly, like a man whose habits of life
have made food less an indulgence than a
necessity. She believed that she was interesting
him.

'My idea in life, my particular form of egoism,
is a determination not to be swamped. I resent

most fearfully, *not* the claims my family make on me, but the claims I make on my family. Theirs are a tribute to my indispensability, mine, a proof of my dependence. Therefore I am a perfectly charming woman, but quite extraordinarily selfish. That is how all my friends describe me. I admire their candour, but I never congratulate them on their perspicacity. My egoism is nothing if not blatant and unblushing.

'Now you go on!' she said encouragingly, helping herself to salad. 'Tell me about your selfishness, then I'll define how it's different from mine.'

He did not appear inspired.

'Yours is a much better kind,' she supplemented. 'Finer. You have given up everything but the thing that won't be given up. In fact, there's nothing wrong in your sort of egoism. It's only your self-consciousness that brings it to life at all. In the middle of your abject and terrible unselfishness you feel a tiny strain of resistance, and it worries you so much that it has rubbed you sore. It's mere morbidity on your part, that's what I condemn about it. Turn your family out into the street and carouse for a fortnight and you'll be a better man at the end of it. Mine is healthy animal spirits, mine is sheer exuberance; yours is a badgered, hectic, unavowed resistance to the people you love best in the world because, unknowingly, you still love yourself better.'

'You wouldn't know the meaning of healthy animal spirits with six children on my income. I suppose what you are trying to say about me, is . . . the turning of the worm?'

'No,' said Marcia, 'not exactly turning. I wonder if I am making a fool of myself? I don't believe you are an egoist at all. My ideas are beginning to desert me; I am really incapable of a sustained monologue on any subject under the sun. You see, generally I talk in circles; I mean, I say something cryptic, that sounds clever and stimulates the activities of other people's minds, and when the conversation has reached a climax of brilliancy I knock down my hammer, like an auctioneer, on somebody else's epigram, cap it with another, and smile round at them all with calm assurance and finality. By that time everybody is in a sort of glow, each believing that he or she has laid the largest and finest of the conversational eggs.

'Goodness, you've finished! Would you just call through the window and ask that woman if there's anything else to eat? She's been taking such an interest in our conversation and our profiles. Say strawberries if possible, because otherwise I have a premonition it will be blancmange.'

The stranger put his head and shoulders through the window. Marcia studied his narrow back in the shabby tweed jacket, his thinning hair and the frayed edges of his collar. One hand gripped the back of his chair; she thought, 'How terrible to see a man who isn't sunburnt.' She listened to his muffled conversation with the waitress, and pushed her plate away, deploring the oiliness of the salad.

With flushed face he reappeared, and two plump arms came through the window after him, removed their plates, and clattered on to the table a big bowl of strawberries and a small greyish blancmange in a thick glass dish.

'I wonder if I'm tiring you,' said Marcia remorsefully. 'I know you came out here to be quiet, and I've done nothing but sharpen my theories on you ever since we made common cause against the coffee-room—it *was* worth while, too, wasn't it? Never mind, I'll let you go directly after lunch, and you shall find the tranquillity you came to look for underneath a lime-tree loud with bees. (I never take the slightest interest in Nature, but I always remember that touch about the bees. I came across it in a book.) I see a book in your pocket. If I wasn't here you'd be reading with it propped up against the water-jug, blissfully dipping your strawberries into the salt and wondering why they tasted so funny. But do let's eat them in our fingers, anyway. I never eat them with a spoon unless there's cream. . . . My husband says he finds me too exhilarating for a prolonged *tête-à-tête*.'

He smiled at her with embarrassment, then leant his elbow on the warm rail of the verandah and looked down on to the road.

'It's so hot,' he said with sudden petulance, 'so beastly *hot*. I didn't realise how hot it was going to be or I wouldn't have bicycled out.'

'It's not very hot here, is it ? Those leaves——'

'No, but I was thinking about the hotness everywhere else. This makes it worse.'

'Fancy *bicycling*. Do let me give you some blancmange; I think it is an heirloom. Did you come far ?'

'From Lewisham.' He added, 'I work in a publisher's office.'

'A publisher—how interesting ! I wonder if you could do anything to help a boy I know; such a charming boy ! He has written a book, but——'

He flushed. 'I am not a—an influential member of the firm.'

'Oh, then, p'raps you couldn't. Tell me, why did you come here to-day? I mean why *here* specially?'

'Oh, for no reason. Just at random. Why did you?'

'To meet somebody who hasn't turned up. He was going to have brought a lunch-basket and we were to have picnicked down by the river. Oh, nobody I shouldn't meet. You haven't blundered into an elopement. I've got no brain for intrigue. After lunch we were going to have sketched—at least, he would have sketched and I should have talked. He's by way of teaching me. We were to have met at twelve, but I suppose he's forgotten or is doing something else. Probably he wired, but it hadn't come before I started.'

'Do you paint?'

'I've got a paint-box.' She indicated a diminutive Windsor and Newton and a large water-colour block lying at her feet.

'I'm sorry,' he said diffidently. 'I'm afraid this must be something of a disappointment.'

'Not a bit.' She clasped her hands on the table, leaning forward. 'I've really loved our lunch-party. You *listened*. I've met very few people who could really listen.'

'I've met very few people who were worth listening to.'

She raised her brows. Her shabby man was growing gallant.

'I am certain,' she smiled, 'that with your delicate perceptions of the romantic you would rather we remained incognito. Names and addresses are——'

'Banality.'

The leaves rustled and her muslins fluttered in a breath of warm wind. In silence they turned their faces out towards the distance.

'I love views,' she said, 'when there isn't anything to understand in them. There are no subtleties of emotion about June. She's so gloriously elemental. Not a month for self-justification, simply for self-abandonment.'

He turned towards her quickly, his whole face flushed and lighted up for speech.

With a grind and screech of brakes a big car drew up under the lime-trees.

Marcia leaned over the verandah rail.

'*John*,' she cried. 'Oh, John!'

She reached out for her parasol and dived to gather up her sketching things.

'How late you are,' she called again, 'how *late*

you are! Did you have a puncture, or what were you doing?'

She pushed back her chair with a grating sound along the tiled floor of the verandah, and stood looking down bright-eyed at his weary, passive, disillusioned face.

'I was right,' she said, 'there are two sorts of egoists, and I am both.'

The Lover

HERBERT PILKINGTON rang the electric bell and, taking a few steps back, looked up to contemplate the house-front. In the full glare of the westerly sun it all looked trim and orderly enough; Cicely had not done so badly for herself, after all, by marrying Richard Evans. Herbert congratulated himself on having foreseen the whole thing from the beginning and furthered it with tact and sympathy. Of course it had been difficult to get poor Cicely off. . . . The hall-door was opened suddenly by Cicely's nervous little maid, who, flattening herself against the passage wall to allow of his entrance, contrived, by dodging suddenly under his arm, to reach the drawing-room door before him and fling it wide.

Richard and Cicely were discovered seated at opposite ends of the sofa and looking very conscious. Cicely wore a pink blouse; she looked prettier than Herbert could have imagined and curiously fluffy about the head. The white-walled drawing-room, dim in the ochreous twilight of drawn blinds, was hung with Richard's Italian water-colours and other pictorial mementos of the honeymoon; it smelt very strongly of varnish, and seemed to Herbert emptier than a drawing-room ought to be. The chairs and sofas had retreated into corners, they lacked frilliness; there was something just as startled and staccato about the room as there was about Cicely and Richard. Poor Mother and Dear Father eyed one another apprehensively from opposite walls; the very tick of the clock was hardly regular.

They always gave one a warm welcome; Cicely was quite effusive, and long Richard Evans got up and stood in front of the fireplace, delightedly kicking the fender.

'*Tea*!' commanded Cicely through the crack of the door; just as she had done at No. 17 and at the New House, during the few short months of her reign there.

'Hot day,' said Herbert, sitting down carefully.

'*Richard's* hot,' said Cicely proudly; 'he's been mowing the lawn.'

'Home early?'

'Well, yes. One must slack off a bit this weather.'

'Idle dog,' said Herbert archly.

'*Doesn't* being engaged agree with Herbert!' cried Cicely, slapping his knee. (She had never taken these liberties at No. 17.) 'Don't you feel wonderful, Herbert? Isn't it not like anything you ever felt before?'

Herbert ran one finger round the inside of his collar and smiled what Doris called his quizzical smile.

'Only three weeks more,' contributed Richard. 'And how's the trousseau getting on?'

'My trousseau?'

'Ha, ha! Hers, of course. My dear Herbert, those dressmaker women have got you in their fist. If they don't choose to let her have the clothes in time she'll put the whole thing off.'

Herbert was not to be alarmed. 'Oh, they'll hurry up,' he said easily. 'I'm making it worth their while. By Gad, Cicely, she does know how to dress.'

'They are most wonderful clothes—she is lucky, isn't she, Richard?'

Herbert beamed complacency. 'She deserves it all,' he said.

'I think she's getting handsomer every day.'

'Happiness does a good deal for us all,' said Herbert gallantly.

'By the way,' said Cicely, winking across at Richard (an accomplishment he must have taught her), 'look carefully round the room, Herbert, and see if you see anyone you know.'

Herbert, who had taken Richard's place on the sofa and was sitting with his hands in his pockets and his legs stretched out, turned his head as far as his collar would permit and made an elaborate inspection of the chimney-piece, the whatnot, the piano-top.

'Very well she looks up there, too,' he said, raising himself a little with arched back for a better view, then relapsing with a grunt of relief. He had seen what he expected, the portrait of his beloved looking out coyly at him from between two top-heavy vases. 'Where did you get that, Cicely?'

'She brought it round *herself*, the day before yesterday. She came in just before supper; I was out, but she stayed a long time talking to Richard. Oh, Richard, look at Herbert getting crimson with jealousy!' Herbert, who never changed colour except after meals or from violent exertion, beamed with gratification. 'Never mind, Herbert,' said Cicely, '*I'm* jealous, too, you see.'

Herbert was often irritated by the way that Richard and Cicely looked at one another across him. He did not enjoy the feeling of exclusion. But of course he and Doris would be able to look at each other across people just like that when *they* were married.

'Do bring it over here, Richard,' said Cicely, nodding at the portrait. 'I want to look at it again.' Tea was carried in, not noiselessly, but quite unnoticed. The brother and sister were looking at the photograph. Herbert leant back, smiling at it with an absent and leisurely pride. Cicely bent forward in eager and short-sighted scrutiny. She seemed to be looking for something in it that she could find.

A young lady with symmetrically puffed-out hair returned both regards from out of a silver frame with slightly bovine intensity. Her lips were bowed in an indulgent smile—perhaps the photographer had been a funny man—a string of pearls closely encircled a long plump neck.

'She has framed it for you very handsomely,' said Herbert. 'I said to her when we were first engaged, "Never stint over a present when it is necessary"—I think that is so sound. "Of course I do not approve of giving indiscriminately," I said, "but when they must be given let them be handsome. It is agreeable to receive good presents, and to give them always makes a good impression."'

Cicely looked guilty; Richard had insisted on consigning the coal-scuttle that Herbert had given them to the darkest corner of the study.

'Doris always understands me perfectly,' continued Herbert, examining the frame to see if the price were still on the back. 'I think it will never be necessary for me to say anything to her twice. If I even express an opinion she always remembers. It's quite extraordinary.'

'Extraordinary,' echoed Richard. His voice had often an ironical note in it; this had prejudiced Herbert against him at first, he seemed rather a disagreeable fellow, but now Herbert knew that it did not mean anything at all. Richard, though not showy-looking, was really a good sort of chap.

Cicely, a little pink (or perhaps it was only the reflection from her blouse), drew up the tea-table and began pouring out. There was a short silence while Richard replaced the photograph; they heard two blue-bottles buzzing against the ceiling.

Richard hacked three-quarters of a new cake into slices, placed the plate invitingly at Herbert's elbow and sat down on a music-stool. Lifting his feet from the floor he rotated idly till Cicely passed him his cup, which he emptied in three or four gulps and put down, then sat gazing expectantly at his brother-in-law.

'Marriage is a wonderful thing,' said Herbert conversationally, recrossing his legs. 'Look at you two now, how comfortable you are. It's all been most successful.'

Cicely had never known till this moment whether Herbert really approved of them.

'The most surprising people,' he continued, 'make a success of matrimony. Of course, people have varying ideas of comfort; everybody does not understand this, therefore there have been, alas, unhappy marriages.'

'But the right people always find each other in the end,' said Cicely dreamily. 'You did sort of feel, didn't you, Herbert, when you first met Doris——'

'Women have these fancies'—Herbert was all indulgence for them—'Doris has confessed to me that she was affected, quite extraordinarily affected, by our first meeting. It made little or no impression upon me. But Doris is a true woman.'

'What *is* a true woman?' asked Richard suddenly. Herbert thought it must be very uncomfortable to live with a person who asked these disconcerting, rather silly questions. He supposed Cicely was used to his ways. Cicely sat stirring her tea and smiling fatuously at her husband.

Herbert, after consideration, decided to turn the question lightly aside. 'I think we all

know,' he said, '*when we find her.*' He wished
Doris were sitting beside him instead of Cicely;
he would have looked at her sideways and she
would have been so much pleased. As it was,
he looked across the table at the bread and
butter, and Richard jumped up and offered
him some more.

'Yes, but what does she *consist* of?' asked
Richard excitedly, forgetting to put down the
plate. Herbert was silent; he thought this
sounded rather indelicate.

'*Sensibility?*' suggested Cicely.

'Infinite sensibility,' said Richard, 'and patience.'

'Contrariness,' added Cicely.

'Inconsistency,' amended Richard.

'Oh *no*. Contrariness, Richard, and weak will.'

Herbert looked from one to the other, supposing they were playing some sort of game.

'She is infinitely adaptable, too,' said Richard.

'She has to be, poor thing,' said Cicely (this
did not come well from Cicely).

'Dear me, Cicely,' interposed Herbert, blinking; 'so you consider women are to be pitied, do
you?'

Cicely opened her mouth and shut it again.
She clasped her hands.

'This does not speak well for Richard,' said

Herbert humorously. 'Doris would be much amused. Now I suppose *Doris* is to be pitied, isn't she?'

'Oh *no*, Herbert,' cried Cicely quickly.

'She doesn't seem unhappy. In fact, I believe there are very few young ladies Doris would change places with at present. And I think you are wrong, my dear Richard; I consider woman most consistent, if she is taught—and she can be easily taught. She is simpler and more child-like than we are, of course. Her way in life is simple; she is seldom placed in a position where it is necessary for her to think for herself. She need never dictate—except, of course, to servants, and there she's backed by her husband's authority. All women wish to marry.'

Richard and Cicely listened respectfully.

'A true woman,' continued Herbert, warming to his subject, 'loves to cling.'

'But she mustn't cling heavily, must she?' asked Cicely.

'She clings not only to her husband but in a lesser degree to her household and'—he coughed slightly—'children. Her sphere——'

'—Is the home,' said Richard quickly. 'But suppose she hasn't got a home?'

'She may now hope till a quite advanced age to obtain a home by matrimony. If she cannot she must look for work. It is always possible for an unmarried woman to make herself useful if she is willing and'—he considered carefully—'bright.'

'Do you like women to be bright?' asked Cicely eagerly.

'It depends,' said Herbert guardedly. He had hated Cicely when she was skittish; it had sat grotesquely upon her as a spinster, though now that she was married a little matronly playfulness did not ill become her. 'Doris is bright, bright and equable.'

Remembering with resentment how uncomfortable Cicely had sometimes made him, he raised his voice a little. 'She has no *moods*. She has simple tastes. She is always very bright and equable.'

'So you really suit each other very well,' summarised Richard, twirling on the music-stool. 'Appreciation is everything to a woman. I congratulate her.'

'Yes,' said Herbert simply. 'But you should congratulate *me*—it is more usual, I think. But we are past all that now; dear me, how many letters there were to answer! And now there are the presents to acknowledge. A very handsome inkstand and a pair of vases came this morning. And in another three weeks we shall be at Folkestone!' . . .

His sister and brother-in-law were so silent that he thought they must have gone to sleep. They were an erratic couple; matrimony seemed to have made them stupid. Richard sat biting his moustache and staring at Cicely, who, with bent head, absently smoothed out creases in the tablecloth. One might almost have said they were waiting for him to go. It was curious how little of this he had suspected in Cicely, although she was his sister. In the evenings he knew that Richard and she read poetry together, and not improbably kissed; through the folding doors he could hear their cold supper being laid out in the dining-room. How could he have guessed that something inside her had been clamouring for these preposterous evenings all her life? She had seemed so contented, sewing by the lamp while he smoked and read the paper and Poor Mother dozed.

It was wasting pity to be sorry for them; he turned from his anæmic relations to review his long perspective of upholstered happiness with Doris. One might almost say that the upholstery *was* Doris. Herbert, feeling his heart grow great within him, could have written a testimonial to all the merchants of Romance. Having given love a trial he had found it excellent, and was prepared to recommend it personally, almost to offer a guarantee. Dear Doris would be waiting for him this evening; demure, responsive, decently elated; he was going to visit at her home. This intention he communicated to Richard and Cicely, who rose in vague and badly-feigned distress. Herbert had said nothing about *going*, as it happened, but since they had so understood him—well, they were scarcely entertaining; he had been there long enough.

They saw him to the gate and stood together under the laburnum tree, watching him down the road. Richard's arm crept round Cicely's shoulders. 'But this, ah God, is love!' he quoted.

And Herbert had forgotten them before he reached the corner.

Mrs. Windermere

In the doorway of Fullers', Regent Street, they came face to face. Mrs. Windermere grasped both Esmée's wrists, drew them towards her bosom, and cried in her deep tremolo, '*My dear*!'

Esmée had not imagined Mrs. Windermere out of Italy. She had never pictured that little pug-dog face without the background of flickering olives, or of velvety sun-gold walls, with cypresses dotted here and there like the exclamation-marks in the lady's conversation. Mrs. Windermere now regarded her with intensity through the long fringes of her hat-brim. She said, 'The same Esmée!' and gently massaged the wrists with her thumbs.

'This is splendid,' said Esmée inadequately, conscious of a rising pinkness and of the long stream of outcoming ladies dammed by their encounter. 'What a funny coincidence!'

'God guided me, dearest!' Mrs. Windermere always mentioned the Deity with confidential familiarity; one felt she had the entree everywhere. 'I meant to have lunched at Stewart's.'

'I'm sorry you've *had* lunch.'

'I will have more,' said Mrs. Windermere recklessly. They pushed their way upstairs and stood over a little table in the window while it was vacated. Esmée untwined the dangling parcels from her fingers and propped up her umbrella in a corner. Mrs. Windermere scanned the menu with the detachment of the satiated, and Esmée confessed that she was hungry. 'Then it must be rissoles,' said her friend enticingly—'little chicken rissoles. I will have a cup of chocolate and an *éclair*.' She gave the orders to the waitress and sat looking at Esmée and tapping a corner of the menu card against her mouth.

'But you don't live in town?'

'No,' said Esmée; 'I'm up for the day. You would have written, wouldn't you, if we hadn't met? I should have been so much disappointed if we'd never——'

'I hope to come and stay with you.'

'That will be lovely,' said Esmée, answering the smile. There was a moment's silence. 'Do you miss Italy?'

'Ye-es.' It was an absent answer; Mrs. Windermere's thoughts were concentrated elsewhere. 'There's something *strange* about you, child,' she said.

Esmée now remembered how her conversation

had been always little rushing advances on the personal. She had a way of yawning reproachfully with a little click of the teeth and a 'Surely we two know each other too well to talk about the *weather*?' if one tried to give the conversation an outward twist. Esmée had found their first walks together very interesting, they had had the chilly, unusual, dream-familiar sense of walking in one's skin. 'There *is* something strange,' said Mrs. Windermere.

'*You* look just the same as ever.'

'There's a stillness here,' said the other, slipping a hand beneath her fur. 'Like the stillness in the heart of the whirlwind. Get right into it, live in your most interior self, and you're unchangeable. You haven't found it yet; you're very young, you've never penetrated.'

'I don't think I have, perhaps,' said Esmée thoughtfully, under the returning influence of Italy. 'Perhaps I rather like *twirling*.'

'Ye-es,' said Mrs. Windermere, leaning back in her chair. Her lustrous eyes looked out mournfully, contentedly, from under pouchy lids, through the long fringes of her hat; her *retroussé* nose was powdered delicately mauve, the very moist lips had a way of contracting quickly in the middle of a sentence in an un-puglike effort to retain the saliva. Curly bunches of grey hair lay against her cheeks, a string of Roman pearls was twisted several times round her plump throat; her furs were slung across her bosom and one shoulder; her every movement diffused an odour of Violet de Parme. She had not removed her gloves, and opulent rolls of white kid encircled wrist and forearm; her sleeves fell back from the elbow. She was an orthodox London edition of her Italian self.

'Twirling,' she repeated, narrowing her eyes. She looked round the mild, bright, crowded room, rustling with femininity, with its air of modest expensiveness. 'Simply twirling? How' —with an obvious connection of ideas—'is your husband?'

'Very well indeed. He would like so much——' Esmée could not picture Wilfred meeting Mrs. Windermere. 'He would have liked to have come up with me to-day,' she concluded.

'Ye-es,' said the other, looking beyond at something. 'How did he ever come to let you go to Italy—alone?'

'I wasn't alone, though, was I? I was with Aunt Emma. Someone had to take her and I'd never travelled.'

'Spiritually, you *were* alone. You were alert,

a-tiptoe, breathlessly expectant. *I* came—but it
might not have been I! How did he come to let
you go like that? Men of his type are not so
generous.'

'But he isn't *that* type.'

The waitress brought the cup of chocolate,
the *éclair* and the rissoles. Mrs. Windermere
stretched out across the dishes, gently disengaged
the fork from Esmée's fingers, and turned her
hand palm upwards on the table.

'That little hand told me everything,' she said.
'And do you know, child, you have his image at
the back of your eyes. I *know* the type—little
loyal person.'

'Wilfred likes me to travel,' said Esmée feebly.
'He finds me rather a tiresome companion when
he wants to talk about places, and you see he
never has time to take me abroad himself.'

'That was a very *young* marriage,' said Mrs.
Windermere, leaning forward suddenly.

'Oh. Do you think so?'

'But you're younger now, after four years of
it. Warier, greedier, more *dynamic*. No children!—*never* to be any children?'

'I don't know.'

'So *wise* and yet *so* foolish.' She sipped delicately the hot chocolate, put the cup down, and
once more slipped her hand under her fur. 'The

Mother-heart,' she said, 'is here. It grows and grows—stretching hands out, seeking, *finding*.'

'I expect there are a great many outlets,' said Esmée, helping herself to another rissole, 'even if one never has any children of one's own. But I hope——'

'What you are seeking,' said Mrs. Windermere firmly, 'is a *lover*.' She took her fork up, speared the *éclair*, and watched the cream ooze forth slowly with a smile of sensual contentment. She had been saying things like this repeatedly, all the time they were in Italy. But they didn't, somehow, sound quite nice in Fullers'. Esmée thought she saw a woman near them looking up.

'I don't think I *am*, you know,' she argued gently, wondering at what date Mrs. Windermere had arranged to come and stay with them.

'Oh, child, *child*. . . . You can't, you know, there's been too much between us. And the Mother-heart knows, you know; the yearning in it brings about a vision. I see you treading strange, dim places; stumbling, crying out, trying to turn back, but always following—the Light.' Mrs. Windermere laid down her fork and licked the cream from her lips. 'And then,' she said slowly, 'I see the Light die out—extinguished.'

There was a pause. 'Thank you very much,'

119

said Esmée earnestly; 'it—it saves a lot to know beforehand. I mean if the Light is going to go out there's something rather desperate about my following it, isn't there? Wouldn't it be——'

'The Light,' interrupted Mrs. Windermere, 'is yours to guard.'

'But wouldn't it be——'

Mrs. Windermere bowed her head and drew her furs together.

'Such a *child*,' she sighed.

'I think I'll have an *éclair* too,' said Esmée timidly. 'Won't you have another one to keep me company?'

'*I*?' started Mrs. Windermere. 'I? *Éclair?* What? Oh well, if it's going to make you *shy*, my watching.'

Esmée ordered two more *éclairs*. 'What,' she inquired, 'are your plans? Did you think of going back to Italy?'

'With the swallows—not before the swallows. I must smother down the panting and the tugging, because my friends can't let me go. They just rise up and say I mustn't. Commands, of course, are nothing, but *entreaties*! Did I tell you in Italy what some people call me?' She laughed deprecatingly and watched the waitress threading her way between the tables with the *éclairs.* 'They call me "The Helper." It sounds like something in a mystery play, doesn't it?'

'Oh yes. It's—it's a beautiful name.'

'It does seem to be a sort of gift,' said Mrs. Windermere, looking beyond her, 'something given one to *use*. You see, I do see things other people can't see, and tell them, and help them to straighten out. Well, take your case. . . . And I've another friend in Italy, the one I was going to stay with after we parted—I don't know if I told you about her? Well, she left her husband. She *grew up*, and found she didn't need him any more. Well, I saw all that for her and was able to help her. I told the other man how things stood—such a manly fellow! He'd been hanging back, not understanding. Well, they went. I bought their tickets for them and saw them off to Italy. They've been having difficult times, but they'll straighten out—I'm still able to help them. I've been staying there a good deal. I *am* able to help them.'

'I suppose they did feel it was the right thing to do,' said Esmée.

'And you,' said Mrs. Windermere, bringing her suddenly into focus. 'What *is* going to happen to *You*? I must come down and have a look at this husband of yours, this Wilfred. Let me see——'

She dived suddenly, her bag was on the floor. She reappeared with it, and its mauve satin maw gaped at Esmée while she fumbled in its depths. Out came a small suède notebook, and Mrs. Windermere, feverishly nibbling the point of the pencil, ran her eye down the pages.

'The twentieth?' she said. 'I could come then if you could have me. If not, the fourteenth of the next, for the week-end—but if I came on the twentieth I could stay longer. Failing the fourteenth——'

Esmée pondered, lowering her lashes. 'I'm afraid, I'm *awfully* afraid it will have to be the fourteenth of next. All this month there'll be Wilfred's relations.'

'Little *caged* thing,' said Mrs. Windermere tenderly. 'Very well, the fourteenth.' She jotted down something in her notebook, looked across at Esmée, smiled, and jotted down some more, still with her head on one side and the little secret smile. 'Ideas, ideas, coming and going. . . . And now! You to your shoppingses and I—well, childie?'

'Please, the bill,' said Esmée to the waitress. 'You *must* let me, please,' she whispered to Mrs. Windermere.

'No, I *don't* like—— Oh well, well. I haven't got a Wilfred. Thanks, dear child!'

They pushed their chairs back and went downstairs together. At the door, Esmée drew a valedictory breath. 'It's been ever so nice,' she said. 'Lovely. Such a bit of luck! And now, I suppose——'

'Which way? Oh, Peter Robinson's? Well, I'll come with you. It doesn't matter about my little shoppingses.'

Firmly encircling Esmée's wrist with a thumb and forefinger she led her down Regent Street.

The Shadowy Third

HE was a pale little man, with big teeth and prominent eyes; sitting opposite to him in a bus one would have found it incredible that there could be a woman to love him. As a matter of fact there were two, one dead, not counting a mother whose inarticulate devotion he resented, and a pale sister, also dead.

The only woman of value to him came down every evening to meet the 5.20, and stood very near the edge of the platform with her eyes flickering along the moving carriages. She never knew from which end of the train he would alight, because, as he told her, it was only by the skin of his teeth that he caught it at all, and he often had to jump in at the nearest open door and stand the whole way down among other men's feet, with his hand against the rack to steady himself. He could have come down easily and luxuriously by the 6.5, in the corner of a smoking carriage, but he gave himself this trouble for the sake of three-quarters of an hour more with her. It was the consciousness of this, and of many other things, which made her so speechless when they met. Often they were through the barrier and half-way down the road before she found a word to say. She was young, with thin features and light hair and eyes, and they had been married less than a year.

When they turned from the road down the tree-shadowed lane he would shift his bag from one hand to the other and steal an arm round her shoulders. He loved her shy tremor, and the little embarrassed way she would lean down to make a snatch at his bag, which he would sometimes allow her to carry. Their house was among the first two or three on a new estate, and overlooked rolling country from the western windows, from the east the house-backs of new roads. It had been built for him at the time of his first marriage, four years ago, and still smelt a little of plaster, and was coldly distempered, which he hated, but they said it was not yet safe to paper the walls.

To-day she said, 'Come down and have a look at the garden, Martin; I've been planting things.' So he put down his bag and they walked to the end of the garden, where a new flower-bed looked scratched-up and disordered, and was edged with little drooping plants.

'Very pretty,' he said, looking at her and absently prodding at the mould with his umbrella. 'I suppose they'll grow?'

'Oh yes, Martin, they're going to grow right up and hide the board-fence; it's so ugly.'

'If they're going to be so tall you should have planted them at the back and put the smaller things in front. As it is, everything else would be hidden.'

'Why, *yes*,' she cried, disheartened. 'I never thought of that—oh, *Martin*! It seemed such a pity to go walking over the new flower-bed, leaving footmarks; that's why I put them near the edge—and now I can't unplant them. What a lot there is to learn! Will you take me to the Gardening Exhibition next summer? I was reading about it—there are corners of gardens by all the famous people, and stone seats, and fountains—we might buy a sundial there, and there are lectures you can go to, and prize roses. We should learn a lot.'

'Next summer? Well, we'll see,' he said. 'Meanwhile don't overdo it—all this gardening.' They skirted the flower-bed and went to lean up against the fence, resting their elbows on the top. She was half an inch taller than he, and her high heels gave her a further advantage. A little wind blew in their faces as they looked out towards the fading distance. The fields were dotted here and there with clumps of elm; with here and there a farmhouse roof, the long roofs and gleaming windows of a factory.

'This open country stretches for such miles,' she said dreamily. 'Sometimes, on these quiet misty days, I begin to think the sea's over there, and that if the clouds along the distance lifted I should see it suddenly, shining. And, with this wind, I could be sure I smell and hear it.'

'Yes, I know. One often gets that feeling.'

'Do *you*?'

'Well, no,' he said confusedly, 'but I'm sure one does. I can imagine it.' Someone had said the same thing to him, just here, three or four years ago.

'You often understand before I say things, don't you, Martin? Isn't it curious? All sorts of woman's discoveries that I've made about this house were nothing new at all to you. Like my idea about a fitment cupboard for that corner of the landing. Fancy that having occurred to you!'

He did not answer. He had taken off his hat, and she watched the wind blowing through his fair hair, as soft and fine as a baby's. Little wrinkles were coming in the forehead that she thought so noble, and his face—well, one could not analyse it, but it was a lovely face. She pictured him swaying for forty minutes in the train, with his hand against the luggage-rack, in order to be with her now, and said, 'Oh, Martin, Martin!'

'Let's come into the house.'

'No, not into the house.'

'Why not? It's cold, you're cold, little woman.' He drew her arm through his and chafed her hand.

'Let's stay out,' she begged. 'It isn't time for supper. It isn't beginning to get dark yet. Do stay out—dear Martin!'

'Why,' he said, looking round at her, 'one would think you were afraid of the house.'

'Hoo!' she laughed, 'afraid of *our* house!'

But he was still dissatisfied. Something was making her restless; she was out in the garden too much. And when she was not in the garden she was always walking about the house. One or two days, when he had stayed at home to work, he had heard her on the stairs and up and down the passages; up and down, up and down. He knew that women in her state of health were abnormal, had strange fancies. Still——

Now she was talking about the new sundial; where they were going to put it. Nasturtiums were to be planted round the foot, she said, because nasturtiums grew so fast and made a show. Her mind had a curious way of edging away from the immediate future. Next summer! Why, she would have other things besides sundials to think of then. What a funny little woman she was!

'I wonder you never thought of having a sundial before,' she insisted. 'Did Anybody ever think of it?'

'Well, no,' he said, 'I don't think it ever occurred to me.'

'Or *Anybody*?'

'No, nor anybody.'

She looked up at the house, silhouetted against the evening sky. 'It's funny living in such a new house—I never had. I wonder who will come after us.'

'We're not likely to move for some time,' he said sharply.

'Oh no—only if we *did*. It seems so very much our house; I can't imagine anybody else at home here, we have made it so entirely—you and I. What was it like the first month or two?'

'Very damp,' he said, now wishing to return to the sundial.

'Did you have the drawing-room very pretty?'

'Oh yes, there were a great many curtains and things. I had to take down all the pictures, they were going mouldy on the walls. It was always a pretty room, even with nothing in it at all. But it's nothing without *you* in it, Pussy.'

'You didn't miss me for a long time,' she said, with her cheek against his.

'Always,' he said, ' always, always, always.'

'Oh no,' she said seriously, 'you know you couldn't have been lonely.'

'*Lonely*—I was wretched!'

'Oh, hush!' she cried with a start, putting her hand over his lips.

'Anyway'—he kissed her fingers—'nobody is lonely now. Come into the house.'

She hung back on his arm a little but did not again protest; they went in by a glass door into the kitchen passage. As they passed through the archway into the hall he put out his hand to sweep something aside; then smiled shame-facedly. It was funny how he always expected that *portière*. *She* had declared that a draught came through from the kitchen, and insisted on putting it up. *She* had filled the house with draperies, and Pussy had taken them down. When the *portière* was there he had always been forgetting it, and darting through to change his boots in the evening would envelop his head and shoulders ridiculously in the musty velvet folds. Funny how he could never accustom himself to the changes; the house as it *had* been was always in his mind, more present than the house as it *was*. He could never get used to the silence half-way up the stairs, where the grandfather clock used to be. Often he found himself half-way across the hall to see what was the matter with it; it had been a tiresome clock, more trouble than it was worth, with a most reverberating tick. Pussy had put a bracket of china there in its place.

Because it was a chilly autumn evening they had lighted a fire in the drawing-room, the cur-tains were drawn; what an evening they would spend together after supper! An armchair had been pulled forward and a work-basket gaped beside it; he wondered what Pussy had been sewing. He stood in the hall, looking in through the open door, and remembered *Her* making baby-clothes by the fire and holding them up in her fingers for him to see. Sometimes he had barely raised his eyes from his book—she had never been able to understand his passion for self-education. As she finished the things she had taken them upstairs and locked them away, and sometimes she would put down her sewing and rattle her work-box maddeningly, and look at him across the fire and sigh. . . . It would be wonderful to watch Pussy sewing. He could hear her moving about in the hall—such a

Pussy!—hanging up his overcoat, then opening the oak chest and rattling things about in it for all the world as though she were after a mouse.

'I found some pictures,' she said, coming up behind him with a stack of something in her arms. 'Come into the drawing-room and we'll look.' The young fire gave out a fitful light, and they knelt down on the hearthrug and put their heads together over the pictures. 'Nursery pictures,' said Pussy—she must have been up in the attic, he wished he had cleared the contents of it out of his house. He stared at the smiling shepherdesses, farmer-boys and woolly lambs. 'They *are* nursery pictures, aren't they, Martin? I didn't know you'd actually bought the *pictures*. Had—had Anybody chosen the curtains, too? Did you get as far as that?'

'I don't know,' he said. 'I don't really, Pussy; I don't remember.'

'And did you take it all to pieces again? Did you alone, or did Anybody help you? I wonder you didn't leave it, Martin; you didn't want the room for anything else. But I suppose it would have made you sad, or other people sad.'

'Have you done anything to the room yet, Pussy?'

'I just pulled the furniture about a little, then I went to look for a fender in the attic and found these pictures. I don't know if there *were* any curtains, Martin; shall I buy some more? I saw some cretonnes specially for that kind of room, all over clowns and rabbits and little scarlet moons.'

'I'll bring some patterns—or come up to town some day and we'll choose them together.'

She did not answer, she was looking at the pictures.

'Martin, was that one going to have been called Martin too, Martin Ralph?'

'I don't know, it hadn't been decided.'

'Didn't Anybody choose a name for him, although he didn't live? He was a real person.'

'It had never been decided, Pussy. I'm going to get you a longer sofa, so that you can put your feet up. We can choose it when we choose the chintzes.'

'Oh, you mustn't. This one is very comfortable; I never sit in it, but that's because I just don't take to it.'

'I hate the look of it.'

'Well, get rid of it,' she said, smiling, 'as neither of us wants a sofa. Did Anybody ever sit on that one?'

As far as he remembered, it was the only thing in the room that she had ever sat on. She had never looked comfortable on it. She had a way

of sitting with her head at the darkest end and
straining her eyes over her work, then blinking
up at him when he spoke. Of course she ought
to have worn glasses; he hated women in glasses,
and she knew it, but her short-sightedness annoyed him and he had frequently said so. *She*
used to come and meet him at the station—he
came back by the 6.5 in those days, sometimes
by the 6.43—and it had so greatly irritated him
to watch her grimacing and screwing up her eyes
at the carriages that he had slipped through the
barrier behind her and pretended when she
came home that he had not known she was there.
Perhaps the little chap would have been short-
sighted if he had lived. . . .

The maid came in to say that supper was
ready, and they went into the dining-room.
Here the curtains were undrawn and they could
see the lights twinkling out in the windows of
the other houses. He often felt as though those
windows were watching him; their gaze was
hostile, full of comment and criticism. The
sound of the wind among the bushes in the garden was like whispered comparisons. He said
they saw a good deal too much of the neigh-
bours, and Pussy said she liked the friendly
lights. 'I wouldn't like to be shut in all round,
but I couldn't live without *any* people. The

next-doors have been so kind. She came in with some plants this morning, and stayed talking quite a long time, and said if there was ever anything she could do. . . . She spoke so nicely of you, Martin. She's known you by sight ever since you were a little boy.'

'Oh, it's funny to have lived in the same place all one's life. All these people—well, they're sometimes rather tiresome.'

'Tiresome?'

'One gets tired of their being the same. Would you like to travel, Pussy?'

'Oh, *Martin*!' Her eyes grew wistful; the prospect seemed remote.

'Well, we will,' he said, with energy. 'We'll go to Switzerland—some summer.'

'I'd rather go to Italy—Venice.'

'Oh, not Venice. I don't think you'd care for Venice. It's nothing very much really.'

'Have *you* been there?'

'Yes, for a bit. I didn't care about it.'

'You never told me!' Her eyes that had been looking into his looked suddenly away, the colour surged up under her clear skin. She began to fidget with the spoons on the table.

'More, Martin?'

'Yes, please—I say, Pussy, you're not eating. You must eat, darling.'

'Oh, I *am*, don't bother. I want to talk.' She lifted her eyes again and glanced at him, the light glinting on her golden eyelashes and on her hair. 'I've been so lonely all day—well, not lonely, but the house was so quiet, I could hear myself think. I went into the east room and sat on the window-seat. It is a cold room; I don't know how we'll ever make it warm enough.'

'It has never been used, you see.'

'We must have fires there this winter. Has it *never* been used? Didn't Anybody ever sit there or go in and out? Oh, they must have, Martin. It's not an empty-feeling room, like the attic.'

'Did you stay there long?'

'No, I didn't, I was feeling restless. The white chest of drawers is locked; I wonder where the key is? We shall be wanting to use it.'

'The key's lost,' he said in sudden fear. 'I know it's lost. I'll go up there some day and force open the drawers myself—they're empty.'

'How funny to lock them if they're empty.'

'What did you imagine was inside?' he asked uneasily.

'Oh, nothing in particular. . . . Martin, I think I will go up to town and buy those chintzes myself. And there are other things I want.'

He remembered how he had heard Her in the

east room those last two months before she went, opening and shutting the drawers. It had disturbed him, working at his desk in the dining-room below, and he had come up angrily once or twice. He could hear Her scuffling to her feet at his approach, and when he entered She was always standing by the window, looking intently out. She used to say, 'Yes, all right. I won't, I'm sorry, Martin,' and come downstairs after him, humming. She had never seemed to have enough to do; before the child came she had been in an aimless bustle, but afterwards she did nothing, nothing at all, not even keep house for him decently. That was probably what had made her ill—that and the disappointment. All the time he had felt Her watching his face; always on the verge of saying something. . . .

When they returned to the drawing-room the fire had burnt down a little. Martin piled on wood, then sat back in the shadow watching Pussy, who, with a reading lamp at her elbow, had begun to sew. He never read these evenings; a table of bric-à-brac had been pushed up against the doors of the bookcase with the gilt-bound classics and encyclopædias which had beguiled his evenings other years. Books, after all, were musty things, and all the book-learning in the world didn't make him more valuable to

Pussy, whose eye wandered when he spoke to her of dynasties or carnivorous plants. He would pull her work-box towards him and amuse himself sorting its contents. One evening he came on a thimble-case which made him start. 'Where did you get that, Pussy?' he asked fiercely. It appeared that she had had it since she was a little girl. Strange that it should be the same as another, so familiar once! He confiscated it and brought her a morocco one next day, with a new thimble in it that did not fit.

This evening, watching her head and hands in the circle of light, he could hardly keep at the other side of the hearthrug from her. She was preoccupied, worked very slowly; at intervals she smoothed out her sewing on her knee, with her head on one side. Pussy was long-sighted, and always looked at things from as far away as possible. When he spoke, her intent eyes fixed themselves on him unseeingly.

'What are you thinking about, Pussy?'

She evidently did not wish to tell him. She smiled, looked round the room a little fearfully, smiled again and took up her work.

'*Pussy?*'

'Oh, I don't know; I'm so happy. I'm so glad to have you back. I wonder if anyone was ever so happy.'

138

'Then why do you look so sad?'

'I was thinking it would be so terrible not to be happy. I was trying to imagine what I'd feel like if you didn't care.'

'*Didn't care!*'

'I—I couldn't imagine it,' she admitted. He could no longer keep the length of the hearthrug between them when she smiled like that. She continued with his arm round her. 'You never let me know the feel of wanting. Just the littlest differences in you would make me eat my heart out. I should never be able to ask you for things. I should just look and look at you, trying to speak, and then you would grow to hate me.'

'—and then?'

'—Don't look at me like that, Martin—and then I should get ill, and if you didn't want me to come back I'd die. . . . Silly, I was only imagining. You shouldn't have made me talk.'

'You shouldn't imagine things like that,' he said sombrely. 'What makes you do it? It's—it's morbid: you might do yourself a great deal of harm. And besides, it's—it's——'

'Do things like that happen? Could a person go on loving and loving and never be wanted?'

'How should *I* know?'

'I think,' she said, 'that not to want a person must be a sort, a sort of murder. I think a person who was done out of their life like that would be brought back by the injustice much more than anybody who was shot or stabbed.'

'Are these the sort of things you think about all day?'

She looked at his white face, and laid her head against his shoulder and began to whimper. 'Oh, Martin, don't be angry. I am so frightened, I am so frightened.'

'Hush!'

'We're not safe and I don't believe we're even good. It can't be right to be so happy when there isn't enough happiness in the world to go round. Suppose we had taken somebody else's happiness, somebody else's life. . . .'

'Pussy, hush, be quiet. I forbid you. You've been dreaming. You've been silly, imagining these horrors. My darling, there's no sin in happiness. You shouldn't play with dreadful thoughts. Nothing can touch us.'

'I sometimes feel the very room hates us!'

'Nothing can touch us,' he reiterated, looking defiantly into the corners of the room.

The Evil that Men do——

AT the corner by the fire-station, where Southampton Row is joined by Theobalds Road, a
little man, hurrying back to his office after the
lunch hour, was run over by a motor-lorry. He
had been stepping backward to avoid a taxi when
worse befell him. What was left of him was
taken to hospital and remained for some days
unidentified, as no papers of any sort were to be
found in his pockets.

The morning after this occurrence a lady
living on the outskirts of a country town received a letter in an unfamiliar writing. The
appearance of the envelope startled her; it was so
exactly what she had been expecting for the last
four days. She turned it over, biting her lip.
The dining-room was darker than usual, it was a
dull, still morning, and she had risen and dressed
with growing apprehension. Her husband was
away, and the windows seemed farther than
ever now that she occupied his place and break-
fasted alone. She poured out a cup of tea and
raised the plated cover of a dish. The sight of a
lonely sausage decided her. She opened the
letter.

Before she had read to the end she leant forward to think, with her knuckles doubled under her chin. Other people have that sinister advantage over one of being able to see the back of one's head. For the first time in her life she had the uncomfortable sense that somebody had done so, that somebody had not only glanced but was continuously staring. Her husband did not make her feel like this.

'Fancy,' she thought. 'Just an hour and ten minutes exactly. Just that little time, and all these years I never knew. Think of living among all these people and never knowing how I was different.'

She folded up the letter for a moment, and began betting against herself on his Christian name. 'Evelyn,' she thought, 'or possibly Arthur, or Philip.' As a matter of fact it was Charles.

'I know you so well,' the letter continued. 'Before you drew your gloves off I knew that you were married. You have been living on the defensive for years. I know the books you read, and what you see in the streets you walk in of that town with the terrible name. You live in a dark house looking over a highway. Very often you stand in the light of the windows, leaning your head against the frame, and trees with dull leaves send the sunshine and shadow shivering over your face. Footsteps startle you, you start back into the crowded room. The morning you get this letter, go out bareheaded into your garden and let the wind blow the sunshine through your hair. I shall be thinking of you then.

'Your husband and your children have intruded on you. Even your children hurt you with their little soft hands, and yet you are as you always were, untouched and lonely. You came slowly out of yourself at that poetry-reading, like a nymph coming out of a wood. You came towards me like a white thing between trees, and I snatched at you as you turned to go back——'

Her cheeks burnt.

'My goodness,' she cried, biting her thumbnail. 'Fancy anybody being able to write like that! Fancy living at 28, Abiram Road, West Kensington. I wonder if he's got a wife, I do wonder.' Delicious warmth crept down her. 'Poetry! I thought he wrote poetry. Fancy him having guessed I read it!'

'I am going to send you my poetry. It is not published yet, but I am having it typewritten. When it is published there shall be just your one initial on the dedication page. I cannot bear the

thought of your living alone among those strange
people who hurt you—familiar, unfamiliar faces
and cold eyes. I know it all; the numb mornings, the feverish afternoons; the intolerable
lamplit evenings, night——'

'Now,' she thought, 'I'm sure he has a wife.'

'—and your wan, dazed face turning without
hope to the first gleams at the window——'

Ah, guilty, guilty, that she slept so well!

The cook came in.

When the meals for the day were ordered and
her breakfast half-surreptitiously eaten with the
letter tucked inside the tea-cosy, she went upstairs to her room and tried on the hat she had
worn in London, folding the side-flaps of the
mirror round her so that she could see her profile. She leant forward gazing at a point in space
represented by the prismatic stopper of a scent-
bottle. With a long, slow breath she went slowly
through the action of drawing off a glove.

'Living,' she said aloud, 'for years and years on
the defensive.' She looked into the mirror at the
neat quiet room behind her, with the reflected
pinkness from curtains and carpet over its white
wall, and the two mahogany bedsteads with their
dappled eiderdowns. There were photographs
of her aunts, her children and her brother-in-
law's wife along the mantelpiece, a print of the

Good Shepherd above the washstand, and 'Love among the Ruins' over the beds. On a bracket were some pretty vases of French china Harold had given her at Dieppe, and a photogravure of the Luxemburg gardens she had given Harold. In a bookcase were several selections from the poets, beautifully bound in coloured suède, and another book, white with gold roses, called 'The Joy of Living.' She got up and slipped a novel from the local library into the bottom of a drawer.

'What on earth would be the good,' she reasoned, 'of going out into the garden when there is no sun and no wind and practically no garden?' She considered her reflection.

'I don't feel I could go down the High Street in this hat. There must be something queer about it. Half-past nine: Harold will be back at half-past eleven. I wonder if he's bringing me anything from London.'

She put a good deal of powder on her face, changed her hat and earrings, selected a pair of half-soiled gloves from a drawer and went downstairs. Then she ran quickly up again and wiped off all the powder.

'Like a wood nymph,' she murmured, 'coming out of a wood.'

When she was half-way down the High Street

she found that she had forgotten her shopping-basket and her purse.

Harold came home at half-past eleven and found his wife still out.

He whistled for some minutes in the hall, looked vainly into her bedroom, the kitchen and the nursery, then went round to the office to put in some work. Harold was a solicitor. Coming in again at lunch-time he met her crossing the hall. She looked at him vaguely.

'Why, you *are* back early!'

'I was back two hours ago,' said he.

'Did you have a nice time in London?'

He explained, with his usual patience, that one does not expect to have a nice time when one goes up to London on business.

'Of course,' he said, 'we're all out to get what we can out of London. We all, as you might say, "pick it over." Only what I'm out for isn't pleasure—I leave that to you, don't I?—I'm out for other pickings.'

'Yes, Harold.'

'This is very good beef.'

'Yes, isn't it?' she cried, much gratified. 'I got it at Hoskins'—Mrs. Peck deals there, she told me about it. It is much cheaper than at Biddle's, tuppence less in the pound. I have to cross over to the other side of the street now when I pass

Biddle's. I haven't been there for three days, and he looks as though he were beginning to suspect——'

She sighed sharply; her interest flagged.

'Ah, yes?' said Harold encouragingly.

'I'm tired of buying beef,' she said resentfully.

'Oh, come, tired of going down the High Street! Why, what else would you——'

She felt that Harold was odious. He had not even brought her anything from London.

'All my day,' she cried, 'messed up with little things!'

Harold laid down his knife and fork.

'Oh, do please go on eating!'

'Yes,' said Harold. 'I was only looking for the mustard. What were you saying?'

'Got any plans this afternoon?' he said after luncheon, according to precedent.

'I'm going to write letters,' she said, pushing past him into the drawing-room.

She shut the door behind her, leaving Harold in the hall. There was something in doing that, 'living on the defensive.' But were there any corners, any moments of her life for the last eight years which Harold had not pervaded? And, horrible, she had not only lived with him but liked him. At what date, in fact, had she ceased liking Harold? *Had* she ever——?

She put her fingers quickly in her ears as though somebody had uttered the guilty thing aloud.

Seating herself at the writing-table, she shut her eyes and thoughtfully stroked her eyebrows with the pink feather at the tip of a synthetic quill pen. She drew the feather slowly down the line of one cheek and tickled herself under the chin with it, a delightful sensation productive of shivers.

'Oh,' she sighed, with a shuddering breath, 'how beautiful, beautiful you are.'

The top of a bus, lurching and rattling through obscurer London, the cold air blowing on her throat, moments under lighted windows when their faces had been mutually discernible, the sudden apparition of the conductor which had made him withdraw his hands from her wrist, their conversation—which she had forgotten. . . . 'Ride, ride together, for ever ride.'
. . . When the bus stopped they had got down and got on to another. She did not remember where they had said good-bye. Fancy, all that from going to a poetry-reading instead of a picture-house. Fancy! And she hadn't even understood the poetry.

She opened her eyes and the practical difficulties of correspondence presented themselves.

148

One could not write that sort of letter on Azure Bond; the notepaper he had used had been so indefinably *right*, somehow. She did not know how to address him. He had not begun with a 'Dear' anything, but that did seem rather abrupt. One could not call him 'Dear Mr. Simmonds' after an hour and ten minutes of such bus-riding; how could you call a person Mr. Simmonds when he said you were a nymph? Yet she couldn't take to 'Charles.' Everything practical, she found, had been crowded into the postscript of his letter—people said that women did that. He said he thought it would be better if she were to write to him at his office in Southampton Row; it was an insurance office, which somehow gave her confidence. 'Dear Charles,' she began.

It was a stiff little letter.

'I know it is,' she sighed, distressfully re-reading it. 'It doesn't sound abandoned, but how can I sound abandoned in this drawing-room?' She stood up, self-consciously. 'The cage that is,' she said aloud, 'the intolerable *cage*!' and began to walk about among the furniture. '—Those chintzes are pretty, I am glad I chose them. And those sweet ruched satin cushions. . . . If he came to tea I would sit over here by the window, with the curtains

drawn a little behind me—no, over here by the
fireplace, it would be in winter and there would
be nothing but firelight. But people of that sort
never come to tea; he would come later on in the
evening and the curtains would be drawn, and I
should be wearing my—Oh, "like a nymph."
How trivial it all seems.'

And Harold had wondered what there would
be left for her to do if she didn't go down the
High Street. She would show him. But if she
went through with this to the end Harold must
never know, and what would be the good of
anything without Harold for an audience?

She again re-read the letter she had written:
'—Of course my husband has never entered
into my inner life——' and underlined the 'of
course' with short definite lines. It was quite
true; she left books of poetry about and Harold
never glanced at them; she sat for hours gazing
at the fire or (as Charles said) out of the window
and Harold never asked her what she was thinking about; when she was playing with the children she would break off suddenly and turn
away her face and sigh, and Harold never asked
her what was the matter. He would go away
for days and leave her alone in the house with
nobody to talk to but the children and the servants and the people next door. But of course

solitude was her only escape and solace; she added this as a postscript.

Harold entered.

'I left this,' he said, 'down at the office this morning by mistake. I thought I had forgotten it in London—I should not like to have done so. I was very much worried. I did not mention the matter as I did not want you to be disappointed.' He extended a parcel. 'I don't know whether it is pretty, but I thought you might like it.'

It was the most beautiful handbag, silver-grey, with the delicate bloom on it of perfect suède—darker when one stroked it one way, lighter the other. The clasp was real gold and the straps by which one carried it of exactly the right length. Inside it had three divisions; drawing out the pads of tissue paper one revealed a lining of ivory moiré, down which the light shot into the shadows of the sumptuously scented interior in little trickles like water. Among the silk folds of the centre compartment were a purse with a gold clasp, a gold case that might be used for either cigarettes or visiting cards, and a darling little gold-backed mirror. There was a memorandum-tablet in an outer pocket, and a little book of *papier poudré*.

They sat down on the sofa to examine it, their heads close together.

'Oh,' she cried, 'you don't mind, Harold? *Papier poudré?*'

'Not,' said Harold, 'if you don't put on too much.'

'And look—the little wee mirror. Doesn't it make me have a little wee face?'

Harold breathed magnanimously over the mirror.

'Harold,' she said, 'you *are* wonderful. Just what I wanted. . . .'

'You can take it out shopping to-morrow morning, down the High Street.'

She shut the bag with a click, brushed away the marks of her finger-tips, and swung it by the straps from her wrist, watching it through half-closed eyes.

'*Harold,*' she sighed ineffably.

They kissed.

'Shall I post your letters?' he inquired.

She glanced towards the writing-table. 'Would you wait a moment? Just a moment; there's an address I must write, and a post-script.'

'My little wee wife,' said Harold contentedly.

'P.P.S.,' she added. 'You must not think that I do not love my husband. There are moments when he touches very closely my *exterior life.*'

She and Harold and the handbag went as far

as the post together, and she watched the letter swallowed up in the maw of the pillar-box.

'Another of your insurance policies?' asked Harold.

'Only just to know the general particulars,' she said.

She wondered for some time what Charles would think when he came to the last postscript, and never knew that Fate had spared him this.

Sunday Evening

It was six o'clock, the dusky sky was streaked with gold behind the beech-trees and the bells were already beginning; they had sat like this since tea. Mrs. Roche had turned half-round to watch the sunset, her hands were clasped along the back of her chair and her chin rested on her interwoven fingers. She blinked a little in the level light, and all the little lines were visible about her eyes and round her puckered mouth. Laura May and Mrs. McKenna sat on the low window seat, faintly aureoled, their empty cups beside them on the floor. Archie Manning was somewhere on the sofa, away among the shadows of the room, leaning back with his legs so twisted that his big feet stuck grotesquely out into the light. They had almost forgotten his existence, and his masculinity did not obtrude itself upon the conversation.

Cups and silver held the last of the sunlight, the tall room gradually obscured itself; here and there a frame or mirror gleamed on the shadowed walls.

They were talking about the First Woman; something had been said of her in the sermon that morning, and the thought had germinated in their minds all day.

Little Mrs. McKenna had had, so far, most to say; now she paused to light another cigarette, and Mrs. Roche turned her eyes in Laura's direction—she did not move her head.

'Laura has been nothing but a dusky profile. What is she thinking about that makes her so silent?'

'Laura is one of these primitive women,' said Mrs. McKenna, inhaling smoke; 'she doesn't think, she communes.'

Laura was a big fair girl; her silences made other people talkative, her virginal starts and blushes stimulated Mrs. McKenna. She sat twisting and untwisting a gold chain round her neck, and said:

'Oh, I don't know really. I am very unoriginal, you know.'

'But nobody is original,' said Mrs. Roche, in her deep voice. 'It's no good, really; all the oldest ideas are the best. But I was thinking, children, looking at the sunset, of her despair, on that first night, watching the light go out of the world. Think how it must have felt.'

'I expect Adam was reassuring,' said Mrs. McKenna; 'he'd seen it happen before.'

'No, he hadn't; they were born on the same

day—that is, weren't they ? Bother, look it up in Genesis.'

'Yes, they were,' said Laura conclusively. She was full of information.

'So Adam had no time to be lonely—that was a pity. It would have made him so much more grateful——'

'—Psychologically,' interrupted Mrs. Roche, 'how interesting it all is, supposing it were true. Eve, of course, was at first no practical assistance to him. There were no chores, no mending. They didn't wear fig-leaves till after the Fall.'

'That must have been nice,' said Mrs. McKenna—'I mean the no fig-leaves. But inexpressive——'

'—Yes, inexpressive. I was going to say, rather impersonal.'

'Oh, come, Gilda, if one's own skin isn't personal, what is !'

'I don't know,' said Mrs. Roche slowly. 'I don't think it's very personal. After all, it's only the husk of one—unavoidably there. But one's clothes are part of what one has got to say. Eve was much more herself when she began putting flowers in her hair than when she sat about in just—no fig-leaves. And she was much more herself than ever when she had got the fig-leaves on, and you and I are much more ourselves than she was.'

'Then do you think covering oneself up is being real?' asked Laura. She entered the conversation with heavy, serious grace, as she would have entered a room.

'I don't know," said Gilda Roche. 'The less of me that's visible, the more I'm there.'

Laura, looking at Gilda's face so nearly on a level with her own, believed that it was one of the dearest on earth, with those satirical eyes. It was in this belief that she came to stay for long week-ends, and was hurt by Mrs. Roche's other incomprehensible friends. 'That's your mind?' she said. 'You mean you feel a deeper sense of identity behind reserve?'

Mrs. Roche looked at her for a moment, then out over her head at the sunset. Mrs. McKenna fidgeted; she disliked this interchange of the personal note. 'I don't agree with you,' she said, raising her voice to drown the insistence of the bells. 'I'm for off with everything—clothes, pose, reserve.'

'Oh, now, Fanny, keep a little pose.'

'Perhaps,' she conceded unblushingly, 'a little. Just a flower in the hair. Then to walk about among things like Eve among the trees, and feel them brushing up against me.'

'But the world is so crowded, Fanny,' said Gilda, who seemed to be enjoying Mrs. Mc-Kenna. 'Just think, wherever you went it would be like walking in the park.'

'I am rather mixed,' said Laura; 'are we speaking metaphorically, or not?'

'*Not*,' said Mrs. McKenna, poking her. 'Oh, decidedly not.' She had been longing to poke Laura for some time, every line of the girl's anatomy annoyed her.

The bells came pealing chime after chime, their echoes pervaded the darkening room. Archie stirred on the sofa.

'Don't they make one feel holy?' he said.

Laura, who had blushed for Archie during the parts of Mrs. McKenna's conversation—one never knew what that little woman was going to say, her mind flickered about like a lizard—thought that it might now be possible to turn the current. 'I like them,' she asserted.

'I hate them! I *hate* them!' cried Mrs. Mc-Kenna, putting her hands up over her ears and stamping her foot.

'They've been ringing for the last half-hour and you didn't seem to mind,' said Gilda Roche, bending down to knock the ash off her cigarette into Laura's tea-cup.

'Yes, but they come in at the pauses so reprovingly; like Wilson putting his owl's face round the door. He longs to clear away the tea-things, but you give him no encouragement, and he is afraid of tumbling over Archie's feet. He's been in three times.'

'I know,' said Gilda penitently. 'But if he takes away the tea-things it will leave us all sitting round in an empty circle, with no particular *raison d'être*.'

'Archie is feeling holy,' said Mrs. McKenna, looking across at the sofa not without respect. 'I wonder what it feels like. At present his mind is in the past. When this present is the past it will linger longest in *this* particular part of the past (how difficult that was to say). Seven or eight Sundays hence, Archie, when you are in Africa, very lonely and primæval, leaning on your gun, you will think back to one Sunday evening in the country, in Gilda's drawing-room, and you'll try and hum the chimes (unconsciously you're learning them now). You'll shut your eyes and see the big windows and the beeches, and Laura and me, and think what sweet women we were.'

'Oh, shall I?' said Archie in a discouraging tone.

Fanny McKenna was coming a little too near the mark; she was a discordant person altogether, and would have been better away. He was very happy with his head in the dark, listening to Gilda and watching Laura listen—he had been curiously attracted lately by the movements of her big head and big, rather incapable-looking white hands.

'I should like a life in the wilds,' said Mrs. McKenna thoughtfully. 'It's a pity I can't go with you.'

'Yes,' said Archie politely.

'But it wouldn't suit me; I should be terrible —luxuriate, over-develop.'

'I thought that was what you wanted, Fanny,' said Gilda unwisely. ' "Off with everything," you know.'

'Not when there was nobody about. What would it matter if everything was off or on? Nobody would be the better for it. What's the good of being sincere when there's nobody to be sincere at?'

'There'd be Archie.'

'Well, anyway, there's William,' said Mrs. McKenna conclusively. 'And I can't go. I'm afraid I don't love Archie enough. But he will be very lonely—won't you, Archie?'

'Oh, I don't know,' said Archie evasively, rolling his head about among the cushions. 'I suppose so. I suppose one will live a good bit in the past and future if one has got too much time to think and not enough to do in the present.'

'What future, Archie?' said Mrs. Roche with curiosity.

'Oh, I don't know. Coming back, I suppose. I ought to be back in four years. I wonder where everybody will be.'

'I shall be here, a little greyer-haired, perhaps, and stupid; several of my friends will have given up coming down to see me, including Fanny—who will be wherever William isn't. Laura will probably be married——'

'Oh?' said Laura consciously.

'—and you will come down once or twice, and be very retrospective and sweet, Archie, then drift away too. Perhaps you will bring the girl you are engaged to down to see me, and she will kiss you on the way home and say I am a dear old thing, and not be the least bit jealous any more. . . . I know I shall be very stupid some day; I can feel it coming down on me, like mist from the top of a mountain.'

'Laura will often come and see you,' consoled Mrs. McKenna, 'and bring all the babies——'

'We must all write to Archie,' interposed Gilda. 'He will never answer, but he will expect the most enormous posts. It's queer that we three who have been talking so much about primæval simplicity should have nothing much in front of us but drawing-rooms and gardens for the next four years, while Archie, who never asks for anything better than a sofa—from all I've seen of him—should be actually going out into the wilds to do things.'

'Why, yes,' said Mrs. McKenna, 'Archie is actually going to revert. Laura would do that easily too. Now for you and me, Gilda, life is much more perilous. Archie and Laura would camp out quite happily, compassed about by a perfect cloud of lions, and so long as they weren't eaten—well, they'd just go on living. But for us the next four years are going to be most terribly dangerous. I have been feeling so happy lately that I know I must be terribly insecure, right at the edge of something. The struggle for life—they'll never know the meaning of it, will they, Gilda? The feeling that if you stopped for a moment you'd go out.'

Gilda's eyes narrowed. 'Yes, it's desperate, Fanny, isn't it? You contesting every inch and I longing to grow old beautifully——'

'And murdering,' said Fanny intensely, 'smothering your youth!'

Gilda began to laugh. 'I don't think you're right in saying that Archie and Laura live—just negatively. They are a great deal more than not

162

dead. And you're very sweeping, Fanny; nobody likes to be dismissed as incomplex. Archie is a man of action, strenuous in his mind, and Laura is reposeful—which needs energy. That is why we love her.'

'Yes, don't we?' said Fanny generously, 'but we can't think how it's done.'

'Oh, all big things are reposeful,' said Gilda; 'look at the beech-trees.'

'I am a very wiry Scotch fir,' said Fanny with relish. 'I stand against the skyline and cry out for gales. When they come I ecstasise. Gilda, you are a larch tree planted in a windy place. You look down and think you long for a valley, but every inch of you undulates. In a calm you'd go quite limp. *You* in a calm——!'

'It's all I want,' said Gilda. She raised her chin from her hands and leant back to look round the shadows of the room, her hands still resting on the back of the chair. She had an eternal youthfulness in gesture and repose. Archie, watching her silhouette against the fading sky, thought she was like a girl of nineteen.

'Hurry, hurry, hurry, hurry!' intoned Fanny suddenly, echoing the church bell, which was now ringing for late comers with a little note of urgency. 'Don't you think we might take

Archie to church? It would give him some more to remember. We might arrive before the second lesson, if we started now, and he could sit between Laura and you in rather a dark pew, and share a book, and sing "Lead, Kindly Light"——'

'Oh, don't, Fanny!'

Fanny had wondered how much of this they were going to stand. She loved to see Gilda defending her lambs. 'Oh, it's only that tiresome little Mrs. McKenna,' she assured them. 'Terribly flippant, isn't she?' She sighed. 'I wonder if anyone will ever think of me on Sunday evenings?'

'Only if they want a fourth at bridge,' said Archie brutally. It was extraordinary how nice boys could hurt.

'I've never been to evening church. I know nothing about it; is it poignant?' asked Gilda. 'Laura, we will go next time you're here.'

'You might go about eight weeks hence,' suggested Archie disinterestedly. 'When I shall be —*there*, you know. It would be rather amusing. And I say, suppose you always write on Sunday evenings—no, of course you couldn't; the house is always full of people. It's awfully funny to think of those bells going, and all these chairs and sofas here, and people in them, and not me.

It's funny to think of everywhere going on without one, and still going on if one never came back.'

'I'll keep your corner of the sofa for you, Archie. No one else shall sit in it.'

'Yes, you might.' The room was getting so dark that it did not matter what one said. Laura leaned back with her head against the window frame and sighed. Fanny, with her arms folded, peered down at her own little feet. Archie began to whistle under his breath. ' "Turn down an empty glass," ' he said.

'Four years will fly,' said Laura.

'All depends,' said Fanny. 'Four years hence——' She shivered.

'Funny if we all met here again,' said Archie.

'We won't,' said Fanny with conviction.

'Who knows, who knows?' said Gilda.

'Who *wants* to know? We'd never dare go on.'

'Oh, Fanny, *dare*? . . . We've got to.'

'We want to,' said Laura quietly.

'Yes, by Jove,' said Archie. 'It's all been jolly good so far; one feels They wouldn't let one down.'

'*They?*' cried Fanny impatiently. 'They *who*? How dependent, how pitiful, how childish!'

'Well, you don't believe we're in the dark for

ever now the sun's gone down,' said Gilda uncertainly.

'We guess it may come up again. We chance it. We're such optimists, such cowards!'

'Well, what do you believe?'

'Believe? I wouldn't *sell* myself.'

'I think *that*'s pitiful,' said Laura.

The door opened.

'Yes, Wilson,' said Gilda, 'I think you might come in and take away the tea.' They heard Wilson fumbling for a moment, then the room sprang into light. They blinked a little, suddenly aware of the furniture, each other's bodies, and a sense of betrayal. Mrs. McKenna rose briskly.

'We might have had some bridge,' she said. 'What a pity some of us can't play.'

She looked down at Laura.

Coming Home

ALL the way home from school Rosalind's cheeks burnt, she felt something throbbing in her ears. It was sometimes terrible to live so far away. Before her body had turned the first corner her mind had many times wrenched open their gate, many times rushed up their path through the damp smells of the garden, waving the essay-book, and seen Darlingest coming to the window. Nothing like this had ever happened before to either her or Darlingest; it was the supreme moment that all these years they had been approaching, of which those dim, improbable future years would be spent in retrospect.

Rosalind's essay had been read aloud and everybody had praised it. Everybody had been there, the big girls sitting along the sides of the room had turned and looked at her, raising their eyebrows and smiling. For an infinity of time the room had held nothing but the rising and falling of Miss Wilfred's beautiful voice doing the service of Rosalind's brain. When the voice dropped to silence and the room was once more unbearably crowded, Rosalind had looked at the clock and seen that her essay had taken four and a half minutes to read. She found that her mouth was dry and her eyes ached from staring at a small fixed spot in the heart of whirling circles, and her knotted hands were damp and trembling. Somebody behind her gently poked the small of her back. Everybody in the room was thinking about Rosalind; she felt their admiration and attention lapping up against her in small waves. A long way off somebody spoke her name repeatedly, she stood up stupidly and everybody laughed. Miss Wilfred was trying to pass her back the red exercise book. Rosalind sat down again thinking to herself how dazed she was, dazed with glory. She was beginning already to feel about for words for Darlingest.

She had understood some time ago that nothing became real for her until she had had time to live it over again. An actual occurrence was nothing but the blankness of a shock, then the knowledge that something had happened; afterwards one could creep back and look into one's mind and find new things in it, clear and solid. It was like waiting outside the hen-house till the hen came off the nest and then going in to look for the egg. She would not touch this egg until she was with Darlingest, then they would go and look for it together. Suddenly

168

and vividly this afternoon would be real for her.
'I won't think about it yet,' she said, 'for fear
I'd spoil it.'

The houses grew scarcer and the roads greener,
and Rosalind relaxed a little; she was nearly
home. She looked at the syringa-bushes by the
gate, and it was as if a cold wing had brushed
against her. Supposing Darlingest were out...?

She slowed down her running steps to a walk.
From here she would be able to call to Darlingest. But if she didn't answer there would be still
a tortuous hope; she might be at the back of the
house. She decided to pretend it didn't matter,
one way or the other; she had done this before,
and it rather took the wind out of Somebody's
sails, she felt. She hitched up her essay-book
under her arm, approached the gate, turned
carefully to shut it, and walked slowly up the
path looking carefully down at her feet, not up
at all at the drawing-room window. Darlingest
would think she was playing a game. Why
didn't she hear her tapping on the glass with her
thimble?

As soon as she entered the hall she knew that
the house was empty. Clocks ticked very
loudly; upstairs and downstairs the doors were a
little open, letting through pale strips of light.
Only the kitchen door was shut, down the end of

the passage, and she could hear Emma moving about behind it. There was a spectral shimmer of light in the white panelling. On the table was a bowl of primroses, Darlingest must have put them there that morning. The hall was chilly; she could not think why the primroses gave her such a feeling of horror, then she remembered the wreath of primroses, and the scent of it, lying on the raw new earth of that grave. . . . The pair of grey gloves were gone from the bowl of visiting-cards. Darlingest had spent the morning doing those deathly primroses, and then taken up her grey gloves and gone out, at the end of the afternoon, just when she knew her little girl would be coming in. A quarter-past four. It was unforgivable of Darlingest: she had been a mother for more than twelve years, the mother exclusively of Rosalind, and still, it seemed, she knew no better than to do a thing like that. Other people's mothers had terrible little babies: they ran quickly in and out to go to them, or they had smoky husbands who came in and sat, with big feet. There was something distracted about other people's mothers. But Darlingest, so exclusively one's own. . . .

Darlingest could never have really believed in her. She could never have really believed that Rosalind would do anything wonderful at school, or she would have been more careful to be in to hear about it. Rosalind flung herself into the drawing-room; it was honey-coloured and lovely in the pale spring light, another little clock was ticking in the corner, there were more bowls of primroses and black-eyed, lowering anemones. The tarnished mirror on the wall distorted and reproved her angry face in its mild mauveness. Tea was spread on the table by the window, tea for two that the two might never . . . Her work and an open book lay on the tumbled cushions of the window-seat. All the afternoon she had sat there waiting and working, and now —poor little Darlingest, perhaps she had gone out because she was lonely.

People who went out sometimes never came back again. Here she was, being angry with Darlingest, and all the time . . . Well, she had drawn on those grey gloves and gone out wandering along the roads, vague and beautiful, because she was lonely, and then?

Ask Emma? No, she wouldn't; fancy having to ask *her*!

'Yes, your mother'll be in soon, Miss Rosie. Now run and get your things off, there's a good girl——' Oh no, intolerable.

The whole house was full of the scent and horror of the primroses. Rosalind dropped the exercise-book on the floor, looked at it, hesitated, and putting her hands over her mouth, went upstairs, choking back her sobs. She heard the handle of the kitchen door turn; Emma was coming out. O God! Now she was on the floor by Darlingest's bed, with the branches swaying and brushing outside the window, smothering her face in the eiderdown, smelling and tasting the wet satin. Down in the hall she heard Emma call her, mutter something, and slam back into the kitchen.

How could she ever have left Darlingest? She might have known, she might have known. The sense of insecurity had been growing on her year by year. A person might be part of you, almost part of your body, and yet once you went away from them they might utterly cease to be. That sea of horror ebbing and flowing round the edges of the world, whose tides were charted in the newspapers, might sweep out a long wave over them and they would be gone. There was no security. Safety and happiness were a game that grown-up people played with children to keep them from understanding, possibly to keep themselves from thinking. But they did think, that was what made grown-up people—queer. Anything might happen, there was no security. And now Darlingest——

This was her dressing-table, with the long beads straggling over it, the little coloured glass barrels and bottles had bright flames in the centre. In front of the looking-glass, filmed faintly over with a cloud of powder, Darlingest had put her hat on—for the last time. Supposing all that had ever been reflected in it were imprisoned somewhere in the back of a looking-glass. The blue hat with the drooping brim was hanging over the corner of a chair. Rosalind had never been kind about that blue hat, she didn't think it was becoming. And Darlingest had loved it so. She must have gone out wearing the brown one; Rosalind went over to the wardrobe and stood on tip-toe to look on the top shelf. Yes, the brown hat was gone. She would never see Darlingest again, in the brown hat, coming down the road to meet her and not seeing her because she was thinking about something else. Peau d'Espagne crept faintly from among the folds of the dresses; the blue, the gold, the soft furred edges of the tea-gown dripping out of the wardrobe. She heard herself making a high, whining noise at the back of her throat, like a puppy, felt her swollen face distorted by another paroxysm.

'I can't bear it, I can't bear it. What have I done? I did love her, I did so awfully love her.

'Perhaps she was all right when I came in; coming home smiling. Then I stopped loving her, I hated her and was angry. And it happened. She was crossing a road and something happened to her. It was angry and she died. I killed her.

'I don't know that she's dead. I'd better get used to believing it, it will hurt less afterwards. Supposing she does come back this time; it's only for a little. I shall never be able to keep her; now I've found out about this I shall never be happy. Life's nothing but waiting for awfulness to happen and trying to think about something else.

'If she could come back just this once—Darlingest.'

Emma came half-way upstairs; Rosalind flattened herself behind the door.

'Will you begin your tea, Miss Rosie?'

'No. Where's mother?'

'I didn't hear her go out. I have the kettle boiling—will I make your tea?'

'No. *No.*'

Rosalind slammed the door on the angry mutterings, and heard with a sense of desolation Emma go downstairs. The silver clock by Darlingest's bed ticked; it was five o'clock. They had tea at a quarter-past four; Darlingest was never, never late. When they came to tell her about *It*, men would come, and they would tell Emma, and Emma would come up with a frightened, triumphant face and tell her.

She saw the grey-gloved hands spread out in the dust.

A sound at the gate. 'I can't bear it, I can't bear it. Oh, save me, God!'

Steps on the gravel.

Darlingest.

She was at the window, pressing her speechless lips together.

Darlingest came slowly up the path with the long ends of her veil, untied, hanging over her shoulders. A paper parcel was pressed between her arm and her side. She paused, stood smiling down at the daffodils. Then she looked up with a start at the windows, as though she heard somebody calling. Rosalind drew back into the room.

She heard her mother's footsteps cross the stone floor of the hall, hesitate at the door of the drawing-room, and come over to the foot of the stairs. The voice was calling 'Lindie! Lindie, duckie!' She was coming upstairs.

Rosalind leaned the weight of her body against the dressing-table and dabbed her face with the big powder-puff; the powder clung in paste to her wet lashes and in patches over her nose and cheeks. She was not happy, she was not relieved, she felt no particular feeling about Darlingest, did not even want to see her. Something had slackened down inside her, leaving her a little sick.

'Oh, you're *there*,' said Darlingest from outside, hearing her movements. 'Where did, where were——?'

She was standing in the doorway. Nothing had been for the last time, after all. She had come back. One could never explain to her how wrong she had been. She was holding out her arms; something drew one towards them.

'But, my little *Clown*,' said Darlingest, wiping off the powder. 'But, oh——' She scanned the glazed, blurred face. 'Tell me why,' she said.

'You were late.'

'Yes, it was horrid of me; did you mind? . . . But that was silly, Rosalind; I can't be always in.'

'But you're my mother.'

Darlingest was amused; little trickles of laughter and gratification ran out of her. 'You weren't *frightened*, Silly Billy.' Her tone changed to distress. 'Oh, Rosalind, don't be cross.'

'I'm not,' said Rosalind coldly.

'Then come——'

'I was wanting my tea.'

'Rosalind, *don't* be——'

Rosalind walked past her to the door. She was hurting Darlingest, beautifully hurting her. She would never tell her about that essay. Everybody would be talking about it, and when Darlingest heard and asked her about it she would say: 'Oh, that? I didn't think you'd be interested.' That would hurt. She went down into the drawing-room, past the primroses. The grey gloves were back on the table. This was the mauve and golden room that Darlingest had come back to, from under the Shadow of Death, expecting to find her little daughter. . . . They would have sat together on the window-seat while Rosalind read the essay aloud, leaning their heads closer together as the room grew darker.

That was all spoilt.

Poor Darlingest, up there alone in the bed-room, puzzled, hurt, disappointed, taking off her hat. She hadn't known she was going to be hurt like this when she stood out there on the gravel, smiling at the daffodils. The red essay-book lay spread open on the carpet. There was the paper bag she had been carrying, lying on a table by the door; macaroons, all squashy from being carried the wrong way, disgorging, through a tear in the paper, a little trickle of crumbs.

The pathos of the forgotten macaroons, the silent pain! Rosalind ran upstairs to the bedroom.

Darlingest did not hear her; she had forgotten. She was standing in the middle of the room with her face turned towards the window, looking at something a long way away, smiling and singing to herself and rolling up her veil.

THE END